Born in the UK, **Becky Wicks** has suffered interminable wanderlust from an early age. She's lived and worked all over the world, from London to Dubai, Sydney, Bali, NYC and Amsterdam. She's written for the likes of *GQ*, *Hello!*, *Fabulous* and *Time Out*, a host of YA romance, plus three travel memoirs—*Burqalicious*, *Balilicious* and *Latinalicious* (HarperCollins, Australia). Now she blends travel with romance for Mills & Boon and loves every minute! Tweet her @bex_wicks and subscribe at beckywicks.com.

Tempted by Her Hot-Shot Doc
is **Becky Wicks**'s debut title

Look out for more books from Becky Wicks
Coming soon

Discover more at millsandboon.co.uk.

For my mum. Sorry about the sex scenes.
Don't tell Dad.

CHAPTER ONE

THE RAIN WAS coming down harder than she'd ever felt it. Sharp, wet pricks to her bare arms sent mini-lightning bolts through Madeline's flesh and deep into her bones as she hurried along the London cobblestones, holding her umbrella over her as best she could.

The bolts, of course, were mostly due to the man her agent had arranged for her to meet—America's wealthiest and most inspiring flying doctor and a man most women would surely kill to meet—Ryan Tobias.

His name, now rolling around in her brain, sent further spikes of adrenaline through her body, along with the goosebumps now settling in with the cold. She'd left in such a hurry she'd forgotten her jacket.

'Don't be late,' Samantha had told her. 'He doesn't like it when people are late.'

But Madeline had been so caught up in her internet research that she'd gone and made herself late anyway. She'd been determined to have as much background information on him as possible before their meeting, and it had been near impossible to tear her eyes away once she'd started.

The internet seemed to have its own busy corner of photos, articles, videos and GIFs made from *Medical Extremes* footage—the show Ryan Tobias starred in along with his team of GPs and surgeons. She'd watched a clip of him walking across the glacier in Alaska to reach a stranded explorer at least five times, pausing on the moment when the camera had gone in for a close-up of his bearded, rugged face in front of the whirring helicopter blades.

She had no idea at all about what Samantha had in mind for her to do with this man, but she couldn't deny it was exciting. And *terrifying*.

Madeline's phone beeped, making her jump. She almost tripped over the cobblestones. Damn, she *had* to pull herself together.

'I'm nearly there,' she blurted hurriedly into it, just as she rounded the corner into Trinity Buoy Wharf.

Samantha was standing there in the doorway, waiting. She was in high heels, too, Madeline noticed. Were they both dressed to impress a man they knew almost never looked impressed?

'He's already here,' Samantha said in a low voice, taking the umbrella and ushering Madeline's wet body through huge green doors into the sandy-coloured building.

A flurry of filming activity assaulted her eyes as she swiped at the raindrops on her skin. Men were everywhere: lifting crates, unscrewing lighting equipment, packing things into cases. It was a studio, as she'd expected, but the hectic feel of the place, plus the knowledge that a good few pairs of eyes were now on her, threw a spanner into her already frazzled works.

'Over here first,' Samantha said, putting a firm hand to Madeline's soaked white shirt and starting off across the room.

She was a little too quick for her to keep up, however, and before she could stop herself her heel was catching on a cable stretched out across the floor. She almost went flying.

'Are you trying to kill yourself?'

The deep voice sounded out in front of her, just as she put her hand to the wall to steady herself.

'I'm so sorry. I'm…' Madeline trailed off, realising it wasn't actually a wall she was touching.

It was hard, undoubtedly, but it was breathing.

'Dr Ryan,' she blurted, straightening up instantly.

She removed her flattened palms from his broad chest, scanned his face up close and felt her cheeks flare from pink to beetroot as her heart started pounding in her ribcage. For a strange moment she felt just as if she'd fallen asleep at her kitchen table and woken up on the YouTube channel.

Ryan Tobias wasn't in his trademark *Medical Extremes* white shirt and jacket. He was wearing a black waterproof coat and jeans. His hair, just as it always was on television, was wild and windswept—as though the breeze over London's River Thames had as little respect for him as the wind in a Patagonian hurricane.

She'd watched *those* clips twice or more. Somehow they'd airlifted a pregnant, sick lady to safety, even though Ryan and the brave pilot had been the only ones willing to risk a flight in the storm.

He was taller than she'd expected, somehow, towering over her with a look of amusement mixed with something she couldn't quite read in his familiar grey eyes.

Madeline realised with horror that he must be taking in her rain-drenched hair and the small but noticeable coffee stain on her shirt. A woman had splashed her latte on her on the tube. What must he be thinking?

She glanced around her. Samantha had been ushered off to another corner and was now apparently deep in what looked like an angst-ridden conversation with a guy waving a flowerpot.

Ryan was still appraising her, she realised.

He coughed and crossed his arms. 'I'm afraid I don't know your name.'

'Madeline,' she said, flustered.

'Where did *you* come from, Madeline?'

'From a *much* less embarrassing situation,' she replied without thinking.

Surprise flickered in his eyes before he uncrossed his arms and laughed. A proper laugh that revealed his teeth, as white as snow-capped mountains—a laugh she was pretty sure she'd heard only two or three times on the television.

'Well, they do insist on blocking the walkways like this,' he said, motioning to their feet. 'Good thing you didn't twist your ankle in those shoes. I don't know which box my emergency supplies are in.'

'Guess I got lucky.'

He threw her a surreptitious half-smile. 'I prefer to live life on the edge of danger, too.'

'I've never seen *you* in high heels.'

She adjusted her handbag on her shoulder as he laughed again. A part of her couldn't quite believe she was making Dr Ryan Tobias laugh.

'Anyway, my agent Samantha, over there, kind of surprised me with all this, so...'

'Your agent?' Ryan's expression shifted before her. 'What do you mean?'

Shards of ice were stuck in his eyes now, and it was as if Madeline was alone with him on the peak of a snowy mountain, or maybe trekking over that glacier to reach another lost adventurer who'd been injured and needed his help. Either way, she was suddenly much colder.

'Agent for what?' His arms were crossed again.

'My writing career.'

His forehead creased into a frown.

'Sorry—sorry.' Samantha bustled up behind her, breaking their locked gazes apart. 'I see you've met Madeline Savoia,' she said, putting a hand to Madeline's shoulder. 'She's almost set to be your new ghost-writer, joining you in the Amazon. What did you think of her portfolio?'

Madeline spun her head around to face Samantha. Ghost-writer? *Amazon?* It was the first she'd heard of it.

Samantha had called her to the TV set at the last minute, saying she had the perfect opportunity for her with none other than the selfless, compassionate and dazzlingly good-looking Ryan Tobias, but she'd assumed she'd be assisting in an interview with him—maybe sending some tweets for the travel and entertainment website Samantha sometimes had her freelance for.

Ryan was unreadable now, standing solid as a rock.

'I see. How much experience do you have with malaria and spider bites, Miss Madeline?'

He didn't sound as friendly as before.

Samantha squeezed her shoulder. 'Madeline is a phenomenal writer, Ryan. You might have read her geopolitical romantic thriller—the one set in Madagascar?'

'Can't say I have,' he said. 'I don't get a lot of time to read.'

He was reading *her*. Madeline knew it. Scrutinising her like a beetle under a microscope. She felt the urge to cover herself, but realised it was pointless.

'She's a keen traveller and explorer, like you, *and* she's a medical professional,' Samantha carried on as Madeline's cheeks flamed. 'I thought she'd be the perfect fit.'

'What kind of medical professional?'

'I used to be a nurse, but I'm not any more...' Madeline let her words taper off. She didn't particularly feel like explaining why she'd quit nursing. The thought of it still shamed her, but she doubted the time she'd spent on the wards of St David's Hospital would help anyone who'd been mauled by a jaguar or hugged by an anaconda in the Amazon.

'Is this necessary, Samantha?' Ryan said, after a moment.

His tone was irritated. His arms were still crossed, tighter than ever.

Something in his icy tone made Madeline recall with a flash the other articles she'd uncovered on the internet. Ryan had lost one of his team members five years ago on a sponsored expedition. He'd been twenty-seven at the time. She remembered thinking that she and Ryan were the same age—both thirty-two now.

No one knew the finer details of how or why the young physician Josephine McCarthy had died suddenly out in the jungle. Ryan had clammed up—never shared it with the media. And the medical team with him at the time had also never divulged what had happened—if they even knew.

The rumour mill had been spinning ever since.

Most of what had been printed was hearsay, of course, but Ryan had spent a lot more time in the wild since then, setting up an HIV awareness programme in Africa, arranging vaccinations at schools in Nepal.

Apparently he hadn't particularly wanted the camera crew to follow him when the concept of *Medical Extremes* had first been discussed, but the money they paid him helped thousands of villages get the medication they needed. And besides, the world needed to see the importance of doctors operating without borders.

That was what had been announced in the press release, at least.

'I'm sorry, Ryan,' Samantha said, interrupting Madeline's thoughts. 'A contract is a contract.'

'I know… I know.'

His jaw twitched in annoyance as Madeline stood awkwardly between them.

'If you don't take Madeline with you we'll only have to send someone else you haven't even met, and we're running out of time.'

'Time has a habit of running out,' he replied, somewhat mysteriously.

He's incredibly moody—that was what she'd read. Those rumours must be true at least. Ryan Tobias spent his life touching the lives of many in the world's most remote locations, but he himself was untouchable. And now Samantha was somehow asking *her* to accompany him on his next televised medical mission to the jungle?

She wondered whether her telling Samantha that she was now single had anything to do with this. She suddenly regretted telling her agent how Jason had decided to pursue his burgeoning relationship with a young zoologist called Adeline.

'How can he want an Adeline when he has a perfectly good Madeline?' she'd said at the time, enraged.

'Ryan!'

Someone was calling him back towards a camera. He didn't move. Instead he shot Madeline a narrow look that rattled every nerve-ending in her body. She fixed her eyes on his, determined not to let him know she had a lump in her throat the size of a cricket ball. He didn't break his gaze—not that she was about to break hers either. She was damned if she'd let another moody man walk all over her, even if he *was* rich and famous.

'Well, as you say, a contract is a contract,' he muttered after a moment, sucking in a breath and letting it out so heavily that Madeline felt her damp hair ruffle.

'It'll be great for your profile,' Samantha told him matter-of-factly, and Madeline caught him rolling his eyes.

'We'll see about that. Good to meet you, Madeline.' He thrust his hand out at her suddenly. 'We can always do with another nurse around, I suppose.'

'Oh, like I said, I'm not a—'

'Ryan! We need you over here, please.' That voice again.

His face was expressionless as he engulfed Madeline's hand with his own, and for some reason another episode of *Medical Extremes* was flashing in her mind. Cambodia. The one where he'd eaten a fried tarantula. It had been a gift from the family of a man he'd helped to save.

Ryan Tobias was fearless—that was what everyone said. Well. She was damned if she'd let him scare her.

'I'm looking forward to working with you,' she said calmly.

'Ryan!'

'I'm *coming*, damn it!'

He dropped her hand, turned and strolled across the studio, and Samantha took Madeline's elbow, leading her to a sofa and coffee table in the corner of the chaos. Both were covered in sheets of paper.

'You did good. I'm so sorry to spring this on you.' She poured them both a cup of coffee. 'But this opportunity wouldn't have waited. I suggested *you* the moment I heard what happened to the last ghost-writer...'

'What happened?' Madeline realised just how dry her throat was.

'Fell down some stairs—cracked three ribs, broke one arm. Ironic isn't the word. Would you like a biscuit?'

She shook her head, glancing to her right. Ryan was walking towards a guy packing a camera into a very large black box on wheels, talking about some supplies he needed but hadn't seen yet. His voice still sent chills… or was it thrills?…straight through her.

Was she *really* going to the Amazon?

'He seems…nice,' she ventured, sipping her coffee.

'He's *very* nice, when everything goes to plan. So, Madeline, the long and short of it is that Ryan's contract states that he needs to deliver a memoir and his publishers want it released for Christmas. Only as yet he's been too busy to write it.'

'OK…'

Madeline gripped more tightly onto her cup and bit into her cheek. Ghost-writing wasn't exactly something she was thrilled about doing. Her last book—written under her own name—hadn't gone too well, though, due to her publisher having no marketing budget, mostly. Her sales had suffered horribly while she'd been out writing the next one in the middle of nowhere in Zimbabwe.

Apparently bad things happened to books if you couldn't spend twenty-four hours a day on Twitter, telling everyone about them.

Bad things happened to relationships, too, if you stupidly left your boyfriend alone for two months…

Madeline pushed thoughts of Adeline from her head.

Samantha sipped her coffee, then put the cup down on the messy table.

'Ryan is about to go and shoot the third season of *Medical Extremes*, as you know, and what with all his appointments he hasn't got time for the memoir, too. We need someone to help him write the book at the same time as he's filming—gather quotes, insights, interviews, you know? Am I right in thinking you're still free to take a week or two, probably three, out of London at the moment?'

Madeline nodded blankly. Ryan was so tall and so commanding without even trying. Everyone seemed to be in awe of him. And although she was a little loath to admit it, after the way he'd just acted towards her, it wasn't hard to see why.

As well as being the sexiest doctor since George Clooney, Ryan was a millionaire who gave selflessly to charities all over the world. He didn't have a lot else to spend his riches on, apparently. His father was a heart surgeon, famed for working with those less fortunate in the US. Ryan had taken things one step further by setting up his own non-profit organisation and flying all over the world with his team, crossing borders to reach people who'd never get help otherwise.

Samantha lowered her voice. 'Ryan doesn't write. Obviously his skills lie in other areas. But with you on board, plus his celebrity status, this book could be a bestseller. Easy. The publishers have a very impressive budget.'

'And Twitter?' Madeline said. 'How many followers?'

'Over four hundred thousand. He never tweets a damn thing, of course, but we have Amy from Middlesex University who's his biggest fan. She won the competition to be his Twitter manager. He just got done with a news team covering the story… BBC, I think. How are *you* at being on camera? You've got great cheekbones—I bet it loves you. And you speak several languages, I recall? Always useful.'

Madeline's stomach lurched. This was turning out to be a lot more than she'd bargained for. But it wasn't as if she had anything else on the cards.

She mused over the offer as Samantha kept on talking. She vaguely registered her agent mentioning Rio, a remote tribe—*'none of those weird neck rings or anything'*—parasites, anaemia… But after a minute she was only half listening, because she could feel Ryan looking at her again from across the room.

She straightened her back again, so that he could see he wasn't intimidating her in any way, and tried to look enthusiastic and excited. She had to play her cards right. This chance was too good to pass up and maybe Samantha was right. It could be a bestseller by Christmas.

We can both get something out of this, she thought, sending the thought across the void and straight into Ryan's cool, iceberg eyes.

CHAPTER TWO

'Did you know that CAN's first pilots were called the flag-bearers of the skies? That was in the early nineteen-forties.'

'I don't know much about CAN at the moment,' Madeline said. 'This was all a bit short notice, as you know. Maybe you could explain?'

She was trying her hardest not to let turbulence affect the way she was talking to Ryan. This plane was far too shaky for her peace of mind, but of course this man flew everywhere for a living and didn't even look as if he'd noticed they were bumping up and down in what felt like God's hugest tantrum since the last giant tornado.

'Correio Aéreo Nacional,' he said, picking up a packet of peanuts and running a tanned thumb over the seal without opening it. 'Their mission was to help integrate the most remote Amazon outposts with the rest of the country.'

'How did they do that?'

Madeline pulled out her notebook, wishing she'd put her laptop under her seat instead of up in the overhead locker. She could type much faster than she could write these days, but there was no way on earth she was climbing past Ryan. She'd rather not risk feeling his eyes on her again as she tripped, or did something else stupid as a result of her nerves.

There was something in his stare, she mused. It stayed with her even with her eyes closed. She'd seen it a thousand times in camera close-ups, of course, and it was part of what drew people in their thousands to watch him in action. It had the power to make you feel like you were the only person on earth. It also had the power to make you feel like an idiot.

Ryan smiled, apparently scrutinising her handwriting from his seat on the aisle. 'CAN transported isolated residents from riverside communities to places where they could be helped—usually the city. They had dozens of planes flying over the Amazon—more than they do now anyway.'

Madeline scribbled as fast as she could to get his words down, feeling thankful that she'd brought a Dictaphone for later.

When she looked up his grey eyes were fixed on her, and she found herself annoyingly self-conscious. At least she wasn't wet and covered in coffee this time— she'd put on a very respectable knee-length blue dress for the flight, one that accentuated her small waist, and she'd left her long hair down around her shoulders. Also, he seemed to be making a concerted effort to be friendly, for which she was more than grateful.

'The flying doctors were known as the Angels of the Amazon, is that right?' she asked him, reaching for her necklace.

'Correct,' he said, watching her fiddling with the silver chain as she slid the small crystal apple up and down on it. 'They *were* angels, Madeline. Still are. They deliver medical aid by aircraft. If they didn't these people would only get help after weeks of travelling on foot through the jungle, or by boat.'

'So, would you consider yourself an angel now, too?'

Ryan frowned, drumming his fingers on his tray table. 'I just do what's necessary—like *they* do,' he said. 'These people live and breathe the Amazon—a place most of us know little about, except that it's a living pharmacy essential to billions of lives on earth, right? They're the caretakers of the jungle and everything in it. By helping them and looking after their health we're helping the environment.'

The plane jostled them again and Madeline's tray table jumped.

'Do you know where we're going?' he asked, catching her notepad before it slid off.

'Caramambatai,' she replied quickly, hoping she was pronouncing it right. 'Your producer says it's an indigenous settlement...'

'The Ingariko tribe, yes. They're spread all over South America, but this camp is pretty much hidden on the border between Brazil, Venezuela and Guyana. It's about as remote as you're going to get. Legend has it people have been swallowed whole by thick morning mists in these parts. They're more likely to have been finished off by surucucu snakes, if you ask me. Highly poisonous, by the way. If you see one it will probably be the last thing you see.'

She realised, now that he was so close, that he had lines around his eyes—proof of laughter, perhaps, more than age. He'd been happy once. Happier than the media made him out to be now anyway. He looked sexier in person, too, she decided.

Then she caught herself.

Sexier? There was no way she was letting herself think

that again. She was here to do a job—and besides, as if *anyone* would go near her, let alone this guy. Her friend Emma had said she reeked of heartbreak, which wasn't particularly nice but was definitely true. Hardly surprising after what Jason had done.

Madeline could still recite every line of that love-struck email to Adeline she'd read by mistake after he'd left his laptop open.

I'm just trying to find the right time to tell her, baby. You know it's not her I'm in love with any more.

'So, how do we reach these people once we get to Brazil?' she asked, trying and failing to cross her legs properly under her tray table.

They'd been on the plane for four hours already, and she'd already counted at least nine things in her head that she'd forgotten to pack or research. She was hoping she'd have time to sort a few things out in Rio—where they were stopping for supplies before taking another flight to Saint Elena.

'We'll take a Cessna,' Ryan said. 'Either that or a Black Hawk—whatever the team have booked. Both are pretty good on the runways.'

'There are runways in the rainforest?'

'Well, they're mud strips, really.'

Ryan opened the peanuts and offered her one. She shook her head, trying her hardest to write without scribbling on the tray table instead. They were still bouncing up and down, as if the plane itself was on some sort of trampoline.

'The runways were carved out by the gold miners initially,' he told her. 'Illegally, of course, but they help us do our jobs so I suppose the *real* value of that gold just keeps on increasing—wherever it is. You can write that down.'

She realised her pen was hovering and that she was lost in thoughts of Jason again. But this time Jason was standing next to Ryan Tobias in the jungle, and being somewhat dwarfed by him.

She blinked to get rid of them both. 'Right, yes. Good idea.' She started to scribble, flustered.

'Whatever you do, stay close to us,' Ryan said suddenly, in a tone that pulled her eyes to his again like a magnet. 'People go missing out there all the time.'

Her breath caught as she saw an emotion she didn't recognise cross his face.

He continued without looking at her. 'Last time we found a burnt-out helicopter which must have crashed twenty years ago. No skeletons inside…who knows what happened to them? The jungle has a way of luring people in and keeping them.'

Madeline tried not to shudder. For some reason she knew he was thinking of Josephine McCarthy. What *had* happened to her, exactly?

'When were you here last?' she asked.

'Eight months ago. Five-day CAN mission. No cameras. We treated six hundred patients for minor infections, brought some ultrasound machines. We felt bad we couldn't help the guy who got shot, though.'

'Shot?'

'He did it to himself—his gun got all twisted. By the time we found him his leg had more larvae in it than a dead horse. We cleaned him out, worked on him a long time, but he didn't make it. So, like I said, don't go wandering off on your own, please.' He met her eyes, concern shining around his pupils. 'And watch what you do with your gun.'

Madeline realised she felt quite ill. 'Ryan, I wouldn't be comfortable with a gun, and I really don't think…'

She trailed off as she caught the smile creeping onto his face and felt her cheeks flush crimson. He was joking.

'Don't worry—you're safe with us,' he chuckled, nudging her gently with an elbow.

But just as quickly as it had appeared his smile was retracted, as if a memory had snatched it back again. Something stopped Madeline asking any more questions, though a million were fizzing on her tongue.

'I *feel* safe with you,' she said instead, meaning it. 'How could anyone not?'

Ryan leaned back against the seat, and looked past her, out of the window again. 'You'll be safe with me as long as you're smart. It's no one's job but your own to protect yourself out here, Maddy. Can I call you Maddy?'

'Sure.'

'The Brazilian military uses these trips to gather intelligence sometimes, so if we have any guests you'll know they're on to something and it's a sign to be on high alert.'

'What do you mean?'

'Cocaine trafficking, illegal gold mining—it's all going on in these parts. There were reports of drug runners in the area not so long ago.'

'Drug runners?' Madeline whispered quietly. 'They wouldn't touch you, though, those sorts of people—would they? Especially not with a TV crew… That would just be drawing attention to themselves.'

Ryan shrugged, pouring a handful of peanuts into his big hand as the clouds fluttered past their window. 'You never know *what* they'll do, but let's just say our carefully made runways are as good for transporting illegal drugs as they are for shifting real medicine. You wouldn't want to see the wrong thing by mistake.'

'Do you ever get scared?'

He seemed to contemplate this for a moment, popping the nuts into his mouth, running a hand over his dark stubble. She studied his lips as he chewed. She'd bet he had a million women after him. She wondered if he'd ever asked anyone out who wasn't some sort of celebrity...

'I wouldn't say I never get anxious,' he replied eventually. 'But if we don't take these risks, Madeline... Maddy...we risk a lot worse. We risk thousands of people dying unnecessarily. Sick people take risks when they hear about us. They walk for days, even weeks, to get our help in these places. If we suddenly decide *we're* too afraid we're failing them and we're failing ourselves. You can write that down, too.'

Madeline put her pen back on her notepad, realising with dismay that her handwriting was worse than a child's.

'So, is there anyone you need to stay in touch with while we're away?' Ryan asked her. 'You know there's no signal in the Amazon? Rio might be your last chance to check in for a while.'

'I'm single. My boyfriend and I broke up,' she said, tucking her hair behind her ear and trying not to let the anger register in her voice.

She'd bypassed the emotional phase a couple of weeks ago and transitioned smoothly into fury—an emotion that reared its head like a lion whenever she thought of Adeline's face. She wished she hadn't checked out the other woman's Facebook page now. It was worse being able to picture her.

'He started seeing someone else while I was away working on my last book. He didn't exactly stop once I got back.'

Ryan was silent. When she looked up he appeared to be fighting a smile.

'I'm sorry to hear that,' he said, straightening his face quickly. 'But I actually meant for this book—do you need to send things to your editor while you're away?'

'Oh.' Madeline's cheeks were on fire. She kicked herself internally. 'Not for a while,' she managed. 'I just have to make sure we get our interviews in—and I'll shadow you, if that's OK.'

'However you think it would work best,' he said, resting his arm on the armrest and brushing hers accidentally. She moved as far away from him as she could, crossing her legs away from him.

'I really am sorry about your boyfriend,' he said quietly. 'It hurts to lose someone you're close with, however you come to part ways.'

Madeline closed her eyes. Something in his voice spoke volumes of his own loss.

'These things happen for a reason,' she said, as firmly as she could manage. She picked up her pen again. 'It'll be interesting to see your work with my own eyes. I've watched most of your shows—you really do amazing things for people.'

'Thanks…we try.' He nodded appreciatively. 'You're a trained nurse, as I recall?'

Her heart sped up. 'Yes, well remembered.'

'Why did you quit?'

She opened her mouth to reply, but shut it again quickly. She found it hard to vocalise exactly what had happened. She'd thrown herself into her writing instead; it was what her counsellor had told her to do.

'It's OK—you don't have to tell me.' Ryan put a hand on top of hers for a moment.

Two seconds, maybe three, of skin-on-skin contact

and her heart was a kangaroo. She yanked her hand back—maybe too quickly. What had happened in the hospital almost poured out of her, but she bit her tongue. He was a relative stranger. And she was in no mood to go into the details of her past life—that was what it felt like sometimes anyway.

For the next few hours Ryan plugged himself into an action movie and left her to read her book. She couldn't help the odd glance in his direction, just to confirm she wasn't dreaming. And she was almost entirely certain he was sneaking a few at *her*. The next few weeks accompanying him and his *Medical Extremes* team were going to be 'extreme', to say the least.

CHAPTER THREE

RYAN STUDIED HIS face in the mirror. He liked to think he didn't really suffer with jet lag any more, but the truth was he probably threw himself head-first into every new time zone without giving his body the chance to react. This mission was going to be a particularly tough one— not least because he'd have Madeline Savoia on his trail.

He rested his hands on the sink, leaned closer to the glass and frowned at his reflection. His eyes looked tired. Madeline had distracted him from sleeping on the plane.

She looked a lot like *her*. The first time she'd all but ploughed into him in the studio he'd almost jumped out of his skin. His reaction had been poor, he knew. Angry... The way he always acted when confronted with something he really had no clue how to handle. He'd felt as if he'd seen a ghost.

Josephine.

The name popped into his head like a gunshot. He swallowed hard, jerked the cold tap on and ran his hand under it. Then he said it out loud, straight into the mirror, watching his lips make their way over the word in a way they hadn't for a long time.'

'Josephine.'

He rarely let her name past his lips. Every time he so much as thought of her the guilt crashed over him like a tsunami. It had smothered him and almost made him tumble when Madeline's hands had pressed against him to steady herself. She hadn't realised, of course, but she'd kind of been holding him up at the same time.

Ryan splashed his face with cold water. The more he tried not to think about this, the more he *did*. It was something about Madeline's eyes. And her pursed lips. And the way she'd crossed her arms defiantly over that coffee stain she'd clearly been so embarrassed about. The way she'd lowered her head just slightly when she'd asserted herself, indicating her vulnerability.

A knock on the hotel room door made him jump again. *Dammit.*

'I'm coming,' he called, wiping his face on the towel and running a hand through his hair. It was getting long at the front again. He frowned at the few stubborn greys now making a permanent home in his stubbled chin.

Nothing he could do about it.

Salt and pepper looks better on you than on my French fries.
#DrRyanTobias

A fan of his had tweeted that the other day. He mentally rolled his eyes—such gushing usually went straight over his head. He had quite enjoyed that French fries reference, though. He liked to think years of torment hadn't marked him physically...at least not as much as they had on the inside.

He threw on a white button-down shirt and pulled on his smartest jeans as the knock sounded out again. 'Give me one second!'

He hopped across the patterned carpet, still doing his belt up, and pulled the door open.

'What's the emergency?'

'No emergency.' Madeline smiled. Her hand was still hovering in the air, as if she was about to knock on his face. 'Sorry to interrupt. You said to knock before I went downstairs.'

'What time is it?' he asked, flustered.

He was totally thrown now. She looked entirely different somehow in this light, with her round, beguiling eyes lined with kohl and a hint of green eyeshadow. His hand found his hair again, at the same time as the other started buttoning up his shirt.

'Almost five thirty,' she told him, with her gaze now fixed on his exposed chest. 'Doesn't the drinks thing start now?'

'Yes, yes—sorry, I got caught up. There was an issue with the supplies being delivered to Saint Elena, and I've been on the phone trying to fix it.'

'Is it sorted out?'

'Almost. I did all I could.'

'OK. Well, don't worry, I'm sure we can sneak you in late without anyone noticing. It's not like you're a VIP or anything.'

Laughter burst from his mouth as he hurried back into the room to pull his shoes out of his suitcase. The dryness in her tone tickled him. He'd always found the British sense of humour quite fascinating.

He grabbed his key card and wallet, turned the bathroom light out and let his eyes travel over Madeline's petite yet curvy figure as he walked towards the door again. She was wearing another dress, an emerald-green one this time, tied around her waist with a paler green belt. Her hair was up now, in a French braid draped over one shoulder, and her lips were glistening in a shade of burgundy.

'Were you writing?' he asked, for want of something to fill the silence.

'In my room? A bit.'

He nodded. He'd fought the urge, on the journey, to ask her more about her books, aware that he'd perhaps been a little rude about her passion before. It was just that when Samantha had first mentioned a ghost-writer he'd imagined for some reason someone older, greyer, crinklier. Perhaps an avid cat-lover or crochet aficionado. He definitely hadn't imagined...well. *This.*

He cleared his throat. 'You look nice,' he said.

'Thank you—so do you.'

'So, you recognise me OK without the *Medical Extremes* outfit?' He smiled now.

'You're kind of hard to miss.'

'Is that right? I thought I'd been watching my weight.'

It was Madeline's turn to laugh now. 'As if you need to. I meant you have presence.'

Ryan realised that her cheeks were redder than they had been five seconds ago. He hadn't exactly intended to get himself dressed in front of her...but, then again, they *were* headed into the jungle. Tribal villages in the Amazon rainforest weren't exactly renowned for their privacy.

He stepped past her, closing the door behind him, then put a hand to the small of her back as they walked towards the elevators, noting her shoes—summer wedges with green straps.

'You're a little better at walking in those,' he said without thinking, pushing the button.

'That tripping over in public thing? That was a one-off—don't worry.'

'I'd only be worried in the Amazon,' he replied as the doors pinged and slid open. 'Big black cables on the floor of the jungle have a nasty habit of not being cables.'

She raised an eyebrow questioningly.

'Snakes,' he explained, and she pulled a face that made him chuckle.

In the elevator, Ryan fixed his eyes on their reflections in the full-length mirror. She was at least a foot shorter than him; that was shorter than— He clenched his fist. This was ridiculous. Madeline was not *her*.

He was determined to count the differences.

Some of her expressions were similar, sure, but Madeline had bigger eyes, wide and unnervingly quizzical—even more so now, framed with make-up. Her hair, long and dark and shiny, was the same…but she was slimmer, perhaps. He didn't know much about women's sizes, but he knew when he could hold a waist with both hands without leaving too much room between his fingers.

The elevator doors swung open. The music in the hotel foyer took the edge off his discomfort slightly as he guided Madeline towards the restaurant, past a crowd of tourists in matching floral shorts, speaking hurried German.

'I'm sure you've been briefed about this,' he said, trying to regain an air of authority if only for his own peace of mind.

'Not really.'

He frowned, looking down into her sea-green eyes, then cleared his throat again. 'Well, this is basically a getting-to-know-you event for the new people joining us and the suppliers. We also have a new cameraman from here in Rio, and a local paramedic. It's about building trust as a team before we get out there, you know? That's when the real work starts.'

'It's a good idea,' Madeline said. 'So I'll introduce myself as your ghost-writer?'

Ryan felt his brow crease. How had he forgotten her

mission? He felt that tsunami again at the thoughts of having to regurgitate any of those moments he'd been trying his hardest to bury for so long—of seeing them laid bare on the pages of a book…a book he'd eventually see someday in a bargain bin, with the forgotten demons that would surely plague him for ever tossed aside by a reader who'd lapped them up and promptly let them go, in a way he never could.

His hand found his hair, swept it from his forehead. 'About this memoir… We need everyone to feel secure in the fact that our attention is fully on the patients. Our work always takes priority.'

'I know that.'

'You're there to write the memoir, of course, but we might need you to help out as a nurse from time to time—'

'I'd really rather not be a nurse while I'm here,' Madeline interrupted.

She paused halfway to the table, where he could see the team already waiting, chatting away. She looked nervous again now.

'Ryan, with all due respect, I didn't come here to—'

'Madeline, I get your current role, believe me, but people will be needing you out there. Do you really think, after everything you've trained for, that you could actually walk away from someone in pain?'

She opened her mouth to respond, but shut it again quickly. Annoyance was flickering in her eyes. He was concerned that this wasn't looking very professional; people were looking at them.

'It's going to be fine,' he whispered in her ear, getting a whiff of her floral perfume as he did so. Dear God, she smelled good.

'Ryan, my man! Good to see you—and who's this?'

The tall, sandy-blond-haired guy approaching them in smart black trousers and a purple shirt was Evan Walker—a trusted friend and doctor from Wisconsin, and a firm voice of reason on the *Medical Extremes* team. Viewers loved him for his sense of humour and equally for his ability to take charge at a moment's notice. He had his own online fan club and was also popular because of his award-winning wife's efforts in setting up a domestic abuse helpline.

'Madeline Savoia is my ghost-writer…for the memoir,' Ryan said calmly as Madeline dutifully held out her hand. 'But she's a nurse, too. I've explained that it's all hands on deck at times.'

He felt her eyes burning his cheek as he spoke, but he didn't turn his head.

'Excellent,' Evan enthused, throwing him a look Ryan knew only he could read. Evan knew everything about Josephine. And he hadn't said a word.

'I'm a huge fan of your work, Dr Walker,' Madeline said.

'Thank you very much. So, have you been out to these parts before?'

A waiter approached and guided them all to their seats.

'No, I can't say I have,' she replied.

Ryan pulled a chair out for her and motioned for her to sit down beside him. He'd noticed the way Evan was looking at her now.

'You know, you really look a lot like…'

'What is there to drink?' Ryan put a hand up for the waiter and signalled for a menu.

Evan seemed to take the hint. He took his seat and started pouring the three of them water from a jug full of ice and lemon.

'You're in for a treat, Madeline,' he continued, 'these

are some of the nicest people on the planet. Always so grateful and patient. It's harsh out there, you know?'

Madeline pulled her glass towards her. Ryan noticed her nails were drumming slightly on the glass. 'So I hear.'

'And they live pretty differently to how we do. Most have no idea that all this is even here, and even if they did they'd probably hate it.' He gestured around him now at the opulent restaurant, with Rio de Janeiro's Ipanema in their direct line of vision through the windows.

Ryan gazed out with Madeline at the swirling cormorants and emerald hills in the distance. The beautiful side of the jungle, he thought to himself, feeling a sudden twinge of familiar guilt.

He forced himself to think of something else.

He couldn't help but wonder yet again what the story was with Madeline quitting nursing. Whenever anyone brought it up she looked as though she might run for the hills. He kind of understood how that felt, though. He'd been running for years.

He'd hidden behind deadlines and responsibilities, creating more work for himself than one man should probably have to deal with in a lifetime. But now it had caught up with him in the form of this woman—sent to spill his secrets to the world.

He motioned to the waiter approaching with the wine. 'White, please,' he said. He turned to Madeline. 'You?'

'Red,' she said. 'Just a bit, though, I don't want to fall asleep at the table. I'm trying to outsmart my jet-lag.'

He smiled.

Evan was still talking. 'Last time we were here we helped a little baby—just nine months old, I think. She had a temperature of one hundred and two and climbing...and she wasn't getting enough oxygen. She had pneumonia...she was malnourished. If we hadn't been there…if *Ryan* hadn't been there…she would have been dead in two days.'

Madeline turned to him as a starter of fresh fruit was placed before her on the table, and he was surprised to notice the glistening of tears in her eyes at the mention of the baby.

Casual conversation about supply checks and sleeping arrangements at the camp kept them going as their starters were consumed and everyone's glasses were refilled, and then, just as the waiters hovered on the periphery with their main courses, Ryan tapped his fork on his glass to silence the table.

He rose to his feet, dropping his napkin.

'Ladies and gents,' he said, smoothing down his white shirt and holding up his glass. 'I'd like to thank you all for coming on this brand-new mission with *Medical Extremes*. Let's welcome Pablo, our new cameraman from right here in Rio, who'll be joining us where thousands wouldn't and hopefully not capturing *everything* on camera. No one looks their best after living on bananas and tropical rain for a few weeks.'

He paused for laughter, which flittered around the table as he'd known it would.

'I'd also like to introduce Madeline, here. She'll be working on some writing and lending a hand wherever possible, so I'd like you all to give her the *Medical Extremes* welcome we give everyone and make her feel like one of the family.'

He raised his glass higher, but before she or anyone could say another word, a noise from the kitchen made the entire room jump in their chairs.

'Fogo! Fogo! Fogo!'

The voice was female.

'Help!'

Ryan just had time to see Evan grab his medical bag before they were both off their chairs in a flash, running for the kitchen. He made it to the back of the restaurant just in time to see the blaze of orange fire running up a woman's sleeve—just before he plunged her arm into a nearby sink, under a gushing tap. She was sobbing.

'What happened?' he asked, and was flooded with a stream of Portuguese. The fire was gone, but a crowd of people in white coats and chef's hats were all talking at once.

Evan was behind him, pulling out a sterile bandage from his bag as Ryan moved closer to keep the woman's arm under the water. It was blistered and red, but he could already tell she wasn't going to need hospital treatment—thank God.

'I'll go tell everyone not to panic—you got this?' Evan said.

'All good,' Ryan told him, and watched him shoot back through the door.

'She was pouring pecans into the chocolate mix when her sleeve caught on fire. That's why they're all over the floor.'

Madeline.

Ryan had only just realised she was there, too. She was holding the bandage Evan had given her and translating every word. He took the bandage from her, noticing the pecan nuts under his feet for the first time.

'She says she's worried the dessert is ruined. It's been cooking too long now without being stirred.'

Ryan listened as Madeline spoke in Portuguese to the crowd and someone moved to stir the pot she was pointing at. She reached for a clean dishcloth, soaked it under another tap and handed it to him. On autopilot Ryan placed it over the woman's arm for a moment, before wrapping the bandage around it and fastening it behind her wrist. Her tears were subsiding already and she really did seem more concerned about her dessert.

'Can you tell her I'll give her some ibuprofen, and that she should go home and get some rest?' he asked Madeline, who promptly did as she was asked.

Back at the table, when the ibuprofen had been dispatched and the drama was all but forgotten, the party resumed its happy chatter while the glorious Rio sunset made way for a sky full of stars.

'You were pretty impressive in there, Nurse Madeline,' he whispered, when he couldn't keep it in any more.

He hadn't been able to stop thinking about it—the way she'd sprung into action and known what to do, and say. His Portuguese was limited, as was his Spanish. He got by—but mostly on charm and miming, he had to admit.

'I didn't do anything,' she said quickly.

He frowned. 'Yes, you did. It was instinctive.'

She shrugged, clearly uncomfortable with his eyes on her. Her jaw started pulsing and he knew not to say anything else.

He also knew without question that keeping away from Madeline Savoia was going to be impossible. Not only was she impossibly intoxicating—whether she liked it or not—she wasn't just a writer.

If he had his way she'd be helping him with medical duties so frequently that the details she really needed for the memoir to be a hit would be the last thing on her mind.

CHAPTER FOUR

THERE WAS SOMETHING about Rio de Janeiro, Madeline decided, that was quite entrancing. The streets were alive with the sound of market stall fruit sellers, and tourists examined cheap patterned sarongs and vibrant paintings of ladies dancing under starry spangled skies. The smell of coconuts and sunscreen permeated the air, and she'd seen more thongs, she mused, in the space of twenty minutes than she'd seen in twenty branches of her favourite high street store back in London.

Madeline had been wandering around in the sunshine for a couple of hours alone, trying to get some last-minute bits and pieces before they were due to catch the plane to Saint Elena at six p.m. The rush of the ocean in her ears as she strolled along the mosaic-riddled promenade, coupled with the whoosh of rollerblades, was like a musical symphony. It was hard to believe that just twenty-four hours ago she'd been climbing out of a black cab in the awful London rain.

Madeline was grateful for this time to herself while Ryan rushed about filming another segment for *Medical Extremes*.

'Go enjoy yourself in the sunshine,' he'd said that morning at breakfast. 'And don't forget Sugar Loaf Mountain.'

She wasn't sure she had the energy for Sugar Loaf. They'd stayed around the table till the early hours last night, discussing the mission they were about to undertake, and perhaps, on reflection, she'd enjoyed a bit too much wine after that incident in the kitchen.

She'd noticed that Ryan had stopped at one glass, and she remembered reading somewhere that Ryan didn't drink much. Something about never knowing when he might need to help someone. She smiled, remembering the look on his face in the kitchen. He hadn't realised she was fluent in Portuguese. Then again, how *would* he have known?

What Ryan had said about her actions being instinctive had been playing on her mind. She'd told herself a million times that her nursing days were over, but he was right. Someone had really needed her and she hadn't been able to turn those instincts off at all.

'Mango!' a fruit seller was calling from her tiny stall.

Madeline shook her head politely. She'd avoided eye contact with Ryan all night after that. She knew without him saying another word that he was planning to demand her nursing skills in the Amazon.

'Pineapple?' another fruit seller called out as she turned another corner.

She smiled once again, holding up the plastic bag of fruit skewers she'd bought earlier.

Ryan had escorted her up to her room at around two a.m. By then she'd been almost asleep on her feet. She'd been acutely aware of his hand on her lower back over her dress as they'd left the dining room, and the sound of him clearing his throat in the elevator as he'd pressed himself against the wall opposite her. She'd felt his eyes on her in the mirror.

She'd pondered at the time that he might be trying to

stand as far away from her as possible in the enclosed space. She'd been doing exactly the same thing.

'Try to sleep in if you can in the morning,' he'd said, stopping with her outside her room. 'It might be the best sleep you'll get for a few weeks. The sleeping arrangements won't be up to this standard in the jungle. But I'm sure you've probably figured that out.'

'I'm looking forward to it,' she'd said, trying to sound as if she meant it. 'Thank you for tonight.'

'Thank *you*,' he'd replied softly.

'We should pencil in some time for us to talk. I was thinking regular slots, maybe one every day...'

'Let me see what I can do once we're out there,' he'd said, cutting her off quickly. 'I mean, of course we have to get this memoir written, but things are going to be really hectic for the first few days at least.'

He'd been looking at the doorframe as he'd said that—not once at her.

'I'll see you tomorrow,' he'd told her, and with that he'd leaned in and dropped a quick kiss on her cheek.

It had been as soft as a moth landing on a shadow. She'd felt the brush of his stubble on her skin, caught a whiff of his cologne. Then he'd turned on his heel and Madeline had watched his undeniably sculpted butt in his jeans as he'd walked the whole way back down the corridor and turned the corner.

For the first time in months, with questions she wanted to ask this mysterious doctor galloping maddeningly through her thoughts along with jet-lag, Madeline had eventually drifted off to sleep without thinking once about her ex. She was grateful for that at least.

Armed with sunscreen and mosquito repellent, plus a new bright yellow sarong and several colouring books and sets of crayons for the children she'd inevitably meet in the Amazon, Madeline reached the hotel again at four p.m.

She'd just arrived back in her room and was planning on changing, packing and heading down to find the team, when a knock on the door made her jump. She went to open it in bare feet, expecting someone from Housekeeping. Her insides performed an impressive somersault as she came face to face with Ryan.

'Hi. Everything OK?' she asked, clutching the door-frame and hoping she didn't look terrible.

'We're still waiting on some of the ultrasound equipment we lost track of yesterday,' he said.

She ran her eyes quickly over his blue denim shirt. The sleeves were rolled up over his tanned forearms and his practical, multi-pocketed khaki trousers made her smile. It was still a surreal dream, being face to face with this man.

She didn't miss him looking her up and down in return, in her knee-length, red strapless sundress. She hoped she hadn't dropped any fruit on it.

'Some of it's already halfway here, so unfortunately it means I'll have to stay another night.'

'Just you?'

'It only needs one of us to wait. The rest of the team will leave today and set up camp as planned. I was just wondering if…'

He trailed off for a second, seeming to contemplate his words. She detected the slightest trace of hesitation.

'I was wondering if you wanted to stay with me? I realise I've been a bit…well, aloof about this whole memoir thing, but I do appreciate you have a job to do. Maybe we can get to know each other a bit better over dinner. If you like. Just us this time.'

Just us this time.

Madeline stood up straighter. 'Yes,' she said quickly. 'I think that would be a good idea—before things get too crazy. Good thinking. I have some questions prepared that will help me get a good head start. I'll think up some more. What time should I meet you?'

She hoped she was sounding professional in this moment, because even as she spoke she was mentally unpacking her suitcase, looking for the right thing to wear to dinner.

Ryan shifted his weight onto his opposite foot and folded his arms. 'I was thinking we'd get out of the hotel. I know a restaurant nearby that does great tapas.'

'My favourite. Huge fan of olives.'

He nodded. 'Good. Shall we say seven in the lobby?'

'Seven it is.'

'Great. Well…' He paused again, uncrossed his arms and let out a long, almost relieved sigh. 'I'll see you then, Maddy.'

She shut the door after him, turning back to her room in a panic. She had precisely three hours to prepare a set of questions that wouldn't make Ryan Tobias fear talking to her about the details they both knew she needed, and in that little time she had to make herself look worthy enough to be out in a restaurant with the world's most famous flying doctor.

She rammed her hands through her hair again.

By the time seven p.m. rolled around Madeline was more or less satisfied that she looked OK. She'd opted for her second-favourite green dress—a casual maxi-dress that plunged at the neck in a V without revealing too much. She'd paired it with a long beaded necklace and left her hair loose around her shoulders. Silver-strapped flat sandals completed the outfit, and a hint of peach lip-gloss made her mouth shimmer in a way she hoped made them look plumper, too.

Gathering her green and silver sequined purse, she put her notebook and pen inside and took one last deep breath before reaching for the door.

Ryan was already waiting for her in the lobby. She felt as if the jet set of the insect world was throwing a party in her stomach as she approached him. She hated being starstruck—if that was what this feeling was. But at least it was taking her mind off her break-up.

'Green is definitely your colour,' he said.

His smile reached his eyes and she could tell it was genuine.

'Thank you.'

Ryan was still wearing his khaki trousers, but had chosen another white button-down shirt that highlighted his broad chest and deep bronze tan. The kind of tan only a travelling man had, she mused in appreciation.

Madeline caught his eyes lingering for a split second on the hint of cleavage she knew she was displaying behind her beads, but instead of feeling self-conscious she realised she was feeling quite empowered.

'Let's go,' Ryan said, patting his flat stomach. 'I'm famished.'

They walked outside together, through the hotel's revolving doors and into the balmy night. The breeze picked up her long hair and tousled it about her shoulders as she walked alongside him.

'Any more news on the supplies arriving?' she asked.

'First thing in the morning, so they said. We'll fly at two p.m.'

They passed a shirtless guitar player on the street—a beaming guy with huge, chunky dreadlocks. Ryan pulled some notes out of his pocket and dropped them into his upturned hat. The guy's hands stopped moving instantly on the guitar frets and his eyes widened at what was clearly a significant amount of money, but Ryan didn't stop.

The palm trees swayed rhythmically to their own calypso as they walked along the street. Tourists strolling towards similar reservations were either hand in hand or holding selfie sticks between them, taking photos. She thought back to her friend Emma's gushing email that morning, posing a million questions and demands of what she wanted Madeline to ask Ryan.

Are you single? seemed to be top of her list.

They were welcomed into the restaurant by a beaming waitress the size of a toothpick, who flicked her long, styled auburn hair over her shoulder as she raked over Ryan with eyes as wide as Bambi's.

'I hope this will be OK for you, sir,' she gushed in a thick Portuguese accent as they were led outside to a table on the terrace. She made a big fuss over arranging Ryan's napkin on his lap.

'Fine, thank you,' he replied, seemingly oblivious to the batting eyelashes an inch from his chest.

Ryan took the wine list. A candle flickered in the middle of the table in a mason jar and Madeline studied his famous face, now bathed in a soft, flattering glow in a way she rarely saw on the television. The surgery lights were always so harsh.

She placed her purse under her feet, careful to keep the strap around her knee. She'd been caught out once by a bag-snatcher in Peru, and these days she was disappointingly quick to suspect passing strangers of crimes they probably had no intention of committing.

All around them people were chatting and laughing amongst themselves and Ryan leaned back in his seat.

'Drink?' he asked. 'You might not get the chance again for a while. They don't have much in the way of vintage wine in the Amazon. How about a cocktail?'

'If you're having one,' she said. 'Or maybe just a gin and tonic?'

'Great idea—make that two, please,' he told the waitress, handing back the drinks menu.

'Coming up. I'll be back to take your food order, Dr Ryan.'

She tottered off on her high heels, and Madeline watched as Ryan took his phone out of his pocket and flipped it to 'silent'.

'Is it not weird that everyone knows who you are?' she asked. 'We're in *Rio*!'

He put his phone back and folded his arms in front of him on the table, unwittingly causing his biceps to bulge in his shirt. 'It's less weird than annoying.'

'I read somewhere that you hardly ever drink,' she followed up, training her eyes away from his biceps.

'That's true. I usually stop at one.'

'In case somebody needs your help and you need to focus?'

He grinned, thumbing the corner of the menu. 'Did you read that online?'

'Maybe.'

'I don't really drink because I choose not to. I guess that's not exciting enough for some people. Anything you don't eat?'

Madeline liked the way he was talking to her. It was *easy*, somehow. She wondered what he'd been like before fame...whether he was different now.

She thought about his question. 'Just coriander. I think you call it cilantro where you're from.'

He smiled. 'Can't stand it either. Tastes like old books.'

'I think it tastes like metal pipes.'

'You've licked a metal pipe?'

'Maybe.'

He was laughing now—she could see his shoulders shaking. 'Well, *there's* a way to start the memoir. *I don't like cilantro and I refuse to dine with people who do—especially if they lick metal pipes, too.*'

She shook her head, laughing with him. 'It has bestseller written all over it.'

They ordered a selection of dishes, and as they chatted idly she scribbled a few notes about his childhood, memories of the years he spent in Chicago looking up to his ambitious yet workaholic father.

'Do you have any siblings?' she asked.

His mouth twitched towards a smile. 'I thought all the basics were on the internet?'

'Some of them, yes, but I'd still prefer to hear it firsthand, from you,' she replied. 'As we've already discovered, people stretch the truth a lot.' She crossed her legs under the table. 'Have you ever looked yourself up on the internet?'

He nodded slowly. 'But it wasn't my smartest move.'

'Why not?'

He pulled a face, leaned back in his seat and turned his glass on the checked tablecloth. '"As we've already discovered, people stretch the truth a lot",' he mimicked. 'But some truths you read and you wish you hadn't.'

'Like messages from your boyfriend to his other woman,' Madeline followed, without even thinking.

She felt her cheeks flush instantly. *Stupid gin.*

When she looked up Ryan was looking at her, his eyes dark now...in shadow. 'Sorry,' she said. 'Still raw, I suppose.'

'Were you together a long time?'

She couldn't look at him now. 'Four years. I thought he was about to propose.'

He exhaled through his nose. 'Damn.'

'To be honest, I haven't had time to think about him since I found out I was coming on this trip. I think I just need to keep busy.'

'Keeping busy helps.'

His tone made her lift her head. As he shifted in his chair she caught that look in his eyes again: a slow burning that unnerved her. Madeline wondered if she should just ask him outright whether he was ready to set the record straight about his team member Josephine McCarthy, but she was forced to close her mouth when the chirpy waitress tottered back over with the first few plates of tapas.

Ryan gestured for Madeline to serve herself a helping of *patatas bravas* and skilfully steered the conversation back to his siblings—one older brother called David, who'd moved to New York and married an art curator, and a younger sister called Monica, who was studying dentistry. Madeline had the feeling Ryan wouldn't be spilling any of his own secrets as quickly as *she'd* just done, even if she asked him outright. Especially not now.

She popped an olive into her mouth. No matter how difficult the mission ahead of her, she refused to be deterred. To think this time last week she'd been wondering how on earth she was going to raise the money she needed to re-do her bathroom. Who knew ghost-writing a book while in the Amazon would wind up paying more than she'd ever earned by putting her own book up on the *other* Amazon?

All she had to do was stay focussed.

CHAPTER FIVE

PILLAR-BOX-RED SUITED Madeline's nails, Ryan thought—although it was going to be pretty damn hard for her to keep any element of her beauty regime going once they got to camp. He'd never let on, but the shine of her hair was also likely to be dulled after a few days of washing it in murky pond water.

He'd felt for her when she'd mentioned her ex. While she amused him with her quirky comebacks, the stabs of pain he sensed in her with certain sentences had an effect on his heart. It seemed that for all of Madeline's bravado in public she was a tiny bit broken.

Not unlike me, he thought with a weary smile.

'So, when did you know you wanted to be a doctor?' she was asking him now.

He leaned further towards her, saw the candle flame between them flickering in her pupils. 'I think I was born knowing I would be.'

'Really? Care to elaborate?'

'Not much—but something tells me I'll have to.'

Madeline raised her eyebrows, putting her pen to her lips. Ryan replied to her questions in as much detail as he could, helping himself to more chorizo and making sure to keep Madeline's plate topped up with her share of the food as she made notes.

He wasn't entirely certain she had the right idea about the food they'd be getting once they reached camp; he didn't know if she had any clue that they'd be on rice, bananas and, if they were lucky, fish the entire time. Either way, he was determined to have them both eat as much as possible now.

He told her how his brother's love of art and the metaphysical had led *him* only to contemplate a career in the physical, and yet the same empathetic streak still rendered them closer to each other than either of them was with their sister.

He explained the cluttered corners of their large family home—the way his mother had diligently cleaned while silently resenting the fact that she had to before wealth arrived and saw to it that she could hire a cleaner—a dumpy, smiley Mexican lady called Rose, who had always jangled with keys and tiny candies for the kids wrapped in foil.

He told her how his mother hoarded books of every genre, and always had a jigsaw puzzle on the go.

'Hmm... I see... I think this would be good in more depth,' Madeline would mutter every now and then. 'Tell me more about your backyard? What trees and flowers grew there in summer? Did you spend much time outdoors?'

He talked and talked, encouraged by her encouragement, until the waitress brought a brand-new candle to replace the one that had sizzled right down to a waxed lump in its jar.

While Ryan was putting on what he thought looked like a pretty good show of wanting to get to work on the memoir, it was really just for Madeline. If Madeline Savoia had turned out to be the crinkly old cat lady of his imaginings he doubted he would have been so accommodating. He definitely wouldn't have been sitting here, opposite her, spilling his family history in a Rio restaurant.

He would have emailed his thoughts in a string of misspelled sentences, probably—last-minute musings thrown together after she had reminded him a hundred times that he was supposed to be helping her. He would have barely seen her, and she'd have sat alone in her room, or in the lobby, drinking coffee and working on her crochet, perhaps.

He'd been selfish with his admissions, with his heart, for years. To the world Ryan was a giving man, generous and kind, but inside he was a tangled mass of secrets that he'd do anything to protect. When they got to the jungle he knew he'd have to remember to keep her busy. He had a feeling she already knew that was his plan. Still, he wouldn't crack.

He wouldn't talk about Josephine.

When the dessert menu arrived she was asking him about his relationship with his mother.

'Mary Tobias, sixty-seven, now married to the ex-head of the Department of Genetic Research and Bioinformatics in Oslo. Is that right?'

'Correct.' He nodded, then ordered a cappuccino from the too-skinny waitress who'd been orbiting them like a satellite since the second they'd arrived.

Even before the television fame and camera crews he'd had no problem attracting attention from the opposite sex, but he'd learnt to be discerning over the years. There had been way too many photographs and way too many tweets.

'Coffee?' he asked Madeline, ignoring the way the waitress was hovering a little too close to him yet again, with her apron ties practically dangling over his shoulder.

'Flat white, please, no sugar,' Madeline said, still scribbling furiously. 'So she still lives in Norway?'

'They travel back and forth. She's good friends with my father, thank God,' he said. 'They're better apart—they were both so driven, so ambitious, they never managed to head anywhere in the same direction. You can write that down.'

'I am. Do you think you're more like your mother or your father?'

He contemplated this, amused at the way she bit her lip or frowned as the sentences took shape beneath her pretty fingers. She was a woman who took great care and interest in what she did—he could tell that already. He wondered if she'd been the same as a nurse and almost brought it up. He decided not to.

'I guess I have my father's drive to help others, and my mother's ambition to see the world,' he said thoughtfully. 'Thankfully I've forged a career that lets me do both.'

'A very successful one,' she followed up. 'Tell me more about your team. How do you choose who comes with you on your missions? Would you say you're as close in reality as you seem on screen?'

He reached out quickly, took the pen from her hand and placed it on top of her notebook. She looked up, surprised.

'I don't think we're there yet, are we?' He held her gaze. He couldn't help notice how she flinched.

'Sorry.'

'I thought we'd go over things in chronological order—my youth, my family, college… Don't you want to hear about my days in the acapella club?'

Her eyes narrowed in amusement. 'Seriously? *That's* not on your Wikipedia page.'

'Of course that's not online. If it was, everyone would

be asking me to sing. My job is to save lives—not to kill people.'

She picked up her pen again. 'I'm sure you're not that bad.'

'Let's just say you can worm your way into a lot of things on looks alone. It was a pretty short-lived experience anyway. I only joined because I had it bad for one of the girls in the group.'

'So you were this handsome in college, too?'

She flushed as she said it, hiding her face behind her hair for a moment, and he did his best to hide his smile. He'd noticed the way she'd been sneaking glances at him, maybe a little starstruck herself. Although he had to admit she was a lot more subtle than a lot of people.

When their coffees arrived he sipped at the hot foam, breathing an internal sigh of relief that he'd diverted her most prying questions and potentially bought himself some time to decide exactly how he was going to keep diverting them once they came around to the elephant in the room. *Could* he get away with a memoir that didn't mention Josephine?

Of course he'd been anticipating questions about her, and he knew he couldn't stop this memoir being written altogether. He didn't have to bare his soul completely, though, did he? He'd kept things light—telling her all about the blonde-haired soprano he'd followed about campus like a puppy dog, before she'd hooked up with the tenor and broke his tone-deaf heart.

By the time they got back to the hotel it was gone eleven p.m., and thankfully Madeline seemed content that her writing was off to a good start. He walked her to her room. The door clicked open at the swipe of her key card and she turned to him.

'Thank you, Ryan, for tonight. It was…fun.'

He kept his hands in his pockets. In this light she looked *less* like Josephine. In fact, with her unique style, Madeline had been morphing since yesterday into her own skin right in front of him. It was getting easier to be around her in that respect…and when their conversation was under control she was easy to talk to, too. She was also incredibly, magnetically beautiful. It wouldn't have taken much to let all his professionalism fly out of the window.

Just for one night.

He cleared his throat. 'It was my pleasure. I doubt we'll get as much one-on-one time once we're at camp.'

He noticed she looked despondent.

'We'll get the job done,' he added, 'and who knows? Maybe you'll have the chance to dust off your nursing skills again.'

'I don't think that will be happening,' she said, clutching at the beads around her neck.

He saw a flicker of a warning in her green eyes—the kind he was already getting to know.

'I know you think it will, but it won't. I'm here solely for the memoir, OK?'

'OK.'

Madeline stepped into her room, turning to face him again in the doorway. He could see her bed, all made up behind her. He rooted his feet to the floor, dug his hands deeper into his pockets.

'Anyway,' she said, 'thank you for dinner.'

'You're more than welcome. It *was* fun. I have to say you make for excellent company, Maddy Savoia, even if you do ask a lot of questions.'

'There are a lot more I *could* ask,' she said, pursing her glossed lips for a second. 'But I have a feeling you're going to make me work for it.'

'It's no fun otherwise.'

He leaned in to drop a kiss on her cheek. He was about to tuck a few stray strands of hair behind her ear when Madeline stepped back from him, putting the doorframe between them.

'Goodnight,' she said curtly, and shut the door.

CHAPTER SIX

THE JUNGLE STRETCHED below them like a deep green blanket and Madeline could imagine a million pairs of eyes on their helicopter—from monkeys to jaguars, bats, rats and snakes, all plotting to lure them in and keep them.

'How are you feeling?' Ryan asked from his seat next to hers.

She turned her head away from the window, her lips a thin line. He put a hand to her arm to reassure her, and she was grateful for his presence. He was dressed in a light blue shirt with the *Medical Extremes* logo on the right pocket and another pair of khakis. She was dressed the same, all the clothes given to her by the producer—only *her* shirt was a tight-fitting tank top.

'You're looking like part of the crew already,' Ryan said loudly over the whir of the blades. 'Are you ready for some flying doctor Amazon action?'

'I don't know how to answer that,' she said honestly, noting the way his hair was sticking out adorably from the sides of his baseball hat. She clutched hard at the notebook on her lap under her seatbelt. Her hair was a mess and she'd long since given up trying to tame the flyaway strands that kept escaping from her ponytail. She assumed she should probably get used to looking dishevelled from this point on.

The flight from Rio to Saint Elena had been fine, but the helicopter now juddering towards the camp was an entirely different story. It was only the second time she'd ridden in one. Jason had taken her on a surprise flight over Manhattan the first time they'd been to New York together, complete with champagne.

Her fingers found the apple on its chain around her neck—a present from her ex on that trip. This helicopter had zero champagne. The box of ultrasound equipment sat strapped in place beside Ryan's feet, and various packages, bags and boxes took up every other inch of space. There was even a box or two of bananas and another labelled 'solar power'.

'Chargers—so we can do it nature's way,' Ryan explained, seeing her studying them. 'We use the sun instead of batteries for a lot of things now...except our phones. Like I said, not much signal out here. Did you make your last-minute calls?'

'A couple,' she said, remembering the one she'd had to make to her insurance company, and also the one she'd sneaked to Emma, during which she'd told her all about the pair of them out in Rio, eating olives and talking about the intricacies of Ryan's childhood.

Emma had squealed so loudly down the phone Madeline had been left with a partially deaf ear for ten minutes.

'But, Maddy, is he *single*?'

'I don't know,' she'd had to admit.

Madeline still felt weird around Ryan. He didn't seem as if he was in a relationship. There had been a moment just before she'd left him lingering in her doorway when she'd suddenly panicked that he was going to kiss her— and not just on the cheek this time. She'd moved away from his face as if she'd been dodging a baseball. It made her hot, just remembering.

But even if they had been flirting a little over dinner there was no way in hell she was about to become another one of his adoring female fans and start looking at him the way that waitress had. Besides, she hadn't kissed anyone like that...like Ryan Tobias...ever.

'We don't just eat those—don't worry—but I'm afraid there won't be too many tapas restaurants...'

'What?' Madeline blinked.

Ryan was still talking. He leaned in closer...so close his nose almost brushed hers as she turned.

'The bananas. Sorry, it's tough to hear over the blades, right?'

'Oh, yeah, a bit. Don't you ever fly these things yourself? I thought I saw you in the pilot's seat in one episode.'

'Sometimes—for kicks,' he said, leaning his head back against the headrest. 'I have my licence, but I prefer to let the professionals do their thing while I do mine.'

'I see.'

'Have you ever flown a plane, Miss City Girl?' he asked, cocking an eyebrow.

'Lots of times! My brother had a radio controlled one. It worked pretty well until he crashed it into a tree in Hyde Park.'

He closed his eyes, faking disparagement. 'Crazy Brits,' he muttered.

But she didn't miss his smile, nor the dimples that had taken to appearing more each time they talked.

At first Madeline had felt like a celebrity, being ushered on board the flight with Ryan Tobias. The new cameraman she'd met at that first dinner at the hotel had followed them, watching every move Ryan made through his viewfinder, his eyes shielded by the rim of his own *Medical Extremes* baseball hat.

She still didn't know how she felt about appearing on camera throughout this mission, but the producer had assured her they wouldn't be making a feature of her. She wouldn't have to talk like the rest of the team, and if she appeared in the show at all she'd appear in the background. All of which went some way towards comforting her, she supposed.

'What do you think of the view from up here?' he asked her. 'Better than Hyde Park?'

A rush of wind ruffled the trees below them like a Mexican Wave as they watched the shadow of the helicopter move like a black eclipse on the canopy.

'It's amazing...' she breathed.

Madeline had seen the rainforest before—in Costa Rica. A very handsome man called Ricardo had dared to capture a poisonous red tree frog, which he'd located by following the sound of its distinct croak. He'd held it in his hands to demonstrate that such frogs were only poisonous at certain times of the year, when they'd eaten a toxic kind of ant.

She'd been fascinated as they'd walked on rope bridges, stretching into the air from lush tree to tree at howler monkey height. She'd felt relatively safe there, above the jungle floor with an experienced guide. Here, however, with an infinite ocean of green treetops disguising what she was sure were a thousand death traps, she was having trouble stopping her stomach from knotting—and they hadn't even landed yet.

'We're heading in, boss,' the pilot called over his shoulder after a few minutes, and when Madeline turned to the window at her side she could finally see a clearing.

They flew in closer. Ryan placed a foot on the box closest to him to stop it moving. Madeline could make out what looked like a thin, long pathway, and two long boats waiting on the murky brown coloured river nearby. The pilot was talking to someone on the ground on the radio, and as the sound of the blades increased her hair whipped up into what she knew with utter certainty would be a mass of unmanageable knots and tangles.

The landing strip was in clear sight now. Two men in knee-length shorts and sleeveless T-shirts were running towards them as Madeline held her hair back out of her face. Three minutes later they were bumping onto the ground in the clearing, gliding to a stop, and Ryan was leaning over her, impossibly close, undoing her seatbelt.

'Home sweet home,' he said.

She watched his big hands on her seatbelt. Her heart-rate spiked even further and she held her breath as her insides tangled like her hair.

One of the men on the ground helped her out of the helicopter with the backpack she'd been given for the trip. It held considerably less than her suitcase. The other man walked with her quickly across uneven ground covered in mud and grass towards the murky-looking water. The swish of the helicopter blades created a welcome fan, but already Madeline could feel the heat closing in on her.

'Sólo tiene que esperar aquí, por favor,' another guy said to her, helping her onto a small boat on the river.

A local, Madeline noted, seeing the black swirling tattoo which stretched all the way up the inside of one arm. He was looking up at the sky.

She replied that, yes, she would wait right there, but when she turned around on her seat she saw Ryan with the pilot, another cameraman she'd been introduced to as Jake and the other man who'd been waiting for them, all lifting each box from the helicopter through a haze of heat wafting up from the ground.

She stepped out of the boat again, walking back towards them. 'Here—I can take those,' she offered, and the pilot shrugged, handing her a box of bananas.

Back at the boat she apologised to the local man whose command she'd disregarded, placed the box carefully to the floor and held her arms out for another, and then another, ignoring the beads of sweat that had started to trickle from her temples.

She didn't miss the look of approval Ryan threw in her direction as he fastened a radio to his belt, but neither did she miss the mosquitoes that were gorging themselves on her blood already.

She put the last box of supplies inside the boat and slapped at the top of her arm as Ryan climbed in beside her.

'You might want to get the DEET out,' he said. 'I trust you've been taking the malaria pills you were given?'

'For three days already—yes, sir.' She reached for the pocket of her backpack. 'Need some?'

Ryan shook his head as she sprayed her arms. 'They don't touch me any more. My blood's not sweet enough.'

She raised her eyebrows. Ryan was sweating, too, but it made *him* look sexy. He lifted the hat he was wearing and swiped at his forehead before stepping to the front of the boat. She realised she'd always loved seeing him all sweaty on the show, and then rolled her eyes at herself. Behind her, the last of the other boxes was being piled into the second boat.

'How far is it to the camp?' she asked, spraying her legs, then shoving the DEET back into her backpack.

'Not far.'

Ryan climbed back over the bench seats to sit beside her. A guy with a long pole stepped on and pushed off from the riverbank with it, quickly leaving the helicopter behind. Madeline couldn't shake the growing sense of apprehension coiling around her like a python. They were literally in the middle of nowhere.

'We need to get to camp soon—that storm's coming fast,' Ryan said beside her.

He was looking at the sky. In the sunlight his eyes were shining under his *Medical Extremes* baseball hat, but she noticed a thick black cloud on the periphery of her vision that definitely hadn't been there when they'd landed.

'I hope the helicopter gets out in time.' He leaned back to rest his elbows on the bench behind them. 'Can you hear that?'

'Hear what?'

'The jungle talking. Gets louder when a storm's on the horizon—they sense it. The insects and the birds...the cicadas and the frogs. The usual volume is loud enough— it sends me to sleep like a lullaby—but I wouldn't trust any of it for a second. Remember what I told you before?'

'I remember. No wandering off on my own.'

'Not even when it looks and seems like the most idyllic place in the world. Promise me?'

She touched a hand lightly to his arm. 'Trust me, I don't want to get eaten by a snake any more than you do. I promise you.'

And then lightning struck somewhere inside her as he took her hand and squeezed her fingers.

'Good,' he said.

His radio made a sound. Madeline watched more insects swirling around them as he dropped her hand and pulled the radio from his belt.

Evan's voice sounded out in the boat. 'How close are you to our dock?'

'Five…ten minutes—what's going on?'

'Emergency—fast as you can. I've called the helicopter back,' came the reply.

CHAPTER SEVEN

THE DOCK WAS a flurry of action as it came into view through the trees. Ryan stood up as the boat drew closer and waved at Evan. He was standing on the edge of the water, supervising the scene. The sky was a dark chalky grey and the wind was raging. The weather could change in a heartbeat in the rainforest—he knew that well—but the timing of this particular storm was supremely unlucky.

'Will we be able to help her?' Madeline asked from behind him.

She'd obviously overheard what Evan had said about a local lady who'd been hurt. She'd been stepping into a boat with a heavy bag of fruit when she'd slipped and hit the metal stairs of the dock with such force that she could no longer move. She needed to be taken to a hospital.

'I hope so,' Ryan told her as their boat pulled up alongside the grassy bank and several guys from the village and the camp helped to pull them in. He felt the rain start to spit on his arms.

'She's still in a lot of pain,' Evan said as Ryan jumped onto the bank.

He ran to the next boat with him and stepped carefully down to go alongside the woman. She looked to be in her fifties, pale and trembling with pain. A man, possibly her husband, was holding her hand beside the makeshift stretcher, looking equally pale. Another of Ryan's volunteers was holding her head and neck in place.

'We've stabilised her. The helicopter can't get to us yet—the wind is too strong.' Evan crouched down beside him. 'We're hoping it's not a herniated disc.'

'Can she feel her legs?' Ryan reached for the woman's other hand. 'I'm here…you're going to be OK,' he told her, before remembering that she probably only understood Spanish. He said it again in broken Spanish and she nodded, then howled out in pain.

'She can feel them, but she says she feels tingling, which isn't good. We've given her some anti-inflammatories, but we don't have any ice.'

'She'll need an MRI,' Ryan said, as the wind screamed like a banshee in his ears.

He was already having flashbacks to what had happened in Patagonia, when the aircraft hadn't been able to take off or land in the storm. He knew Evan probably was, too.

Before he knew it Madeline was stepping down beside him, carrying something—a plastic sheet from their boat. She handed him one corner, motioning for him to make a cover with it to put over the woman.

'Thank you,' he said, moving fast to tie it up.

Madeline took the other end, just as a cameraman appeared from nowhere and started capturing their every move.

'This rain's going to get worse,' he said.

'Can I do anything else?' she asked, as he watched a huge raindrop cruise down her nose.

'You can round up all these spectators and get them out of here,' Evan replied, pointing at the crowd, still watching, all agog. 'We need everyone out of here so the helicopter can land.'

As he spoke, the wind picked up yet another notch and rocked the boat, but Madeline was already climbing back up to the riverbank, calling out in Spanish.

'Is there any language she can't speak?' Evan said to Ryan, half laughing in spite of the situation. Ryan shrugged, but inside he was reeling. So much for the nurse who didn't want to be a nurse.

Evan's radio buzzed again. Ryan glanced up at Madeline, now herding people out of the clearing. He could see some of his crew moving quickly to help her. She didn't seem particularly fazed that they'd only just arrived in the middle of nowhere and a first-class storm was building up strength around them.

'The helicopter's managed to take off,' Evan said in relief. 'We'll have to take her to Manaus—it's the closest.'

A tree creaked close by in the wind and Ryan felt the woman grabbing his hand even harder as she wailed again. She was in so much pain but there was nothing more they could do right now. She needed ice—which they didn't have—and it was important to keep her conscious, so she could recount what she was and wasn't feeling. He prayed to God it wasn't a herniated disc, or worse.

Eventually the helicopter whirred into sight, scattering the leaves on the ground around them. Thunder crashed in the distance, and then came even closer, almost drowning out the noise of the blades. Ryan looked on in dismay as he realised it might be too windy for it to land.

Madeline was running towards them again now and his heart lurched at the sight. 'Get out of the way!' he yelled at her, realising how unsteady in the sky the helicopter was.

But Madeline was still running—right underneath it.

His heart almost stopped as the helicopter lurched and then lifted again. She reached them, panting. She was soaked through, but was holding some cushions from the camp. Ryan grabbed her arm, pulling her into the boat, under the plastic shelter they'd created.

'What were you *doing*?'

'She'll need these—there was nothing else around here that I could see...'

'I said don't do anything stupid—weren't you listening?' His hand was still around her arm as the helicopter finally descended in the clearing behind them.

Her eyes were wide, incredulous. 'It wasn't anywhere near me! The pilot saw me!'

'Goddammit, Maddy.'

'I'm *helping* you! I thought that was what you wanted?'

'She is helping us,' Evan confirmed, before motioning to the volunteer and Ryan to help him lift the stretcher carefully out from under the shelter.

It was very humid and the thunder crashed again, just after a bolt of lightning lit up the sky. The pilot turned off the engine.

Ryan dropped Madeline's arm. 'Let's go!' he yelled at Evan, and together they moved as quickly and smoothly as they could, while the woman continued to moan, wail and whimper.

Madeline was with them, speaking in quick Spanish, trying to comfort her, hurrying beside them in the rain.

They were all but drowned rats by the time they made it to the helicopter, but Ryan noticed Madeline didn't flinch or look away from the woman once. They loaded her and her husband into the back of the helicopter in the thrashing rain, taking one seat out in order to make the stretcher fit.

'Are you OK to go?' Ryan asked Evan.

He knew he would be of better use to the people at camp, and he realised that he didn't want to leave Madeline. God knew what else she might try and do.

'Of course, doc,' Evan said, climbing into the back with another cameraman.

The volunteer got into the front and Ryan pulled Madeline back against him as the engine started up again, her hair whipping his face.

'Wait—take these,' she said, breaking free and handing Evan the cushions.

He took them appreciatively and used them as padding around the woman's side, still being careful not to move her. Ryan knew she'd be moved anyway, thanks to the juddering of the helicopter in this weather. He wasn't entirely sure it was a good idea to fly, but some risks were worth taking. The heat and humidity in the jungle tended to accelerate people's injuries.

He guided Madeline away quickly by the elbow as the blades began to whir again. They turned around just in time to see the helicopter rise, then drop back onto the grass.

Madeline gasped.

'Damn,' Ryan cursed. 'They can't take off in this storm.'

'She needs a hospital,' Madeline said.

'I know, but we'll just have to wait it out. It won't last long—these storms never do. Where's our stuff?'

'My bags and yours? They were taken to the camp.' She brushed her wet hair back from her face with her hand.

'Go find them and get warm and dry—there's nothing else you can do.'

He wanted her safe. Not out here in the middle of a storm. He was already viewing her as a liability. He knew it was unfair of him, but Madeline Savoia definitely had a stubborn streak. He watched as she turned and did as he'd ordered, albeit reluctantly, and felt some modicum of relief as one weight at least was lifted from his shoulders.

It took what felt like an eternity to get the helicopter off the ground, and when Ryan made it through to his team he was wet and shivering himself. The camp was a frenzy of action, and as he signed some documents on a clipboard thrust suddenly under his nose he noticed Madeline helping someone to move the boxes of bananas and the other stuff that had obviously been moved in from their boat.

'Ryan, how did it go?'

It was Mark Bailey—up in his face, forcing his eyes away from her. Mark was a young doctor who'd been with them for three seasons of *Medical Extremes*. He was well liked around the place—and even more so on Instagram.

'They're en route to the hospital—finally. Fingers crossed the storm doesn't start up again.'

'Looks like it's stopping,' Mark said.

'No other emergencies so far?'

Ryan adjusted his hat as he walked with him, trying not to look at Madeline again. He was surprised she was out of her tent. She was talking to people and he hadn't even made any introductions yet. Then again, she did seem to be a person who took the initiative. Sometimes too *much* initiative.

'A couple this morning—one sprained wrist and a spider bite. Steady trickles for general check-ups and queries all day. We know the other villagers are making their way over now word that we're here has spread up the river, so we're leaving Maria stationed for any strays tonight and planning on an early start tomorrow.'

'Good call.'

Ryan was glad for Mark's organisational skills, as well as everything else. He noticed that the producer was approaching Madeline, leading her away behind one of the stations.

The camp comprised four stations. One was simply a raised platform, on which stood three foldable tables. There his team doled out vitamins and basic medication, and assessed the symptoms of those seeking other medical attention. Everyone who needed care went there first. With the rain and the storm there were only three people in the line now, waiting to be seen.

The other three stations were for treatment, so they held a couple of beds and chairs, with boxes of fresh sheets, gauze and other equipment stacked in all corners.

Would Madeline know what to do with all this, from her nursing days? he wondered. He knew he had to think of more tasks for her. He'd witnessed her instinctual need to help on more than one occasion now, and all this might make her tired...perhaps too tired to ask for many details for that memoir...

He clenched his fists to his sides as Josephine's face flashed before his eyes.

Don't think about it.

In one of the stations one of his volunteers from Chicago—a fifty-something half-Japanese lady called Maria—was talking to two young children on a plastic sheet on the floor. The kids were young members of the local tribe, no older than seven years old. Often the kids in these remote places gathered around out of excitement at having new people to play with.

'Good to see you, Ryan,' Maria called out, and the barefoot children giggled and waved in their ragged, faded clothing.

He waved back. Then, content that his staff had everything under control, he turned in the direction of the sleeping quarters. The rain was only spitting now.

He found Madeline unpacking her bags, hunched over on the floor of her small green tent.

'Did you find the mini-bar OK?' he asked from the canvas doorway.

She turned around in surprise, still on all fours. The tent wasn't exactly big enough to stand up in.

A sheen of perspiration was causing her face to glisten and her long wet hair was stuck in strands to the side of her face. She obviously hadn't yet found time to get dried off. She got to her knees, swiped at her forehead and gestured around her.

'Five-star,' she said, smiling. Then her expression changed. 'How's that patient? Do you think she'll be OK?'

'They're on the way to the hospital—we'll know more once they do some tests,' he said. He cleared his throat. 'Thank you for your help. I'm sorry if I sounded a little harsh back there. You...you freaked me out for a second.'

'Why?'

'You can't just run under helicopters, Maddy. You're not Indiana Jones.'

She grimaced. 'Sorry, I didn't think. And, yes, the mini-bar is well stocked, thanks.' She reached for a bottle of water that was poking out of her backpack and held it up.

Her tent, which had been set up prior to her arrival, complete with sleeping bag, blankets and a prized inflatable mattress, was luxurious compared to where most of the people in the tribe and surrounding villages slept.

'We have someone covering emergencies for now,' he told her, 'but with any luck things will be slow until the morning.'

'Great—well, maybe we can work on the memoir some more?' She stepped out of the open doorway and stood beside him. 'Where are you sleeping?'

He looked behind him. No one was around. 'Want to see?'

'OK.'

He led them past a line of tents—all for the crew—and past the makeshift fire they often gathered around in the evenings. The rain was less impactful there, thanks to the thickness of the leaves and branches overhead, but the wind was still muttering all around them. He put his pack on the mossy floor, crouched down and pulled out his prized possession. Holding it in his hands he stood and looked around, studying his surroundings.

'Where to go…? Where to go…?'

'Where to go with what?'

Madeline looked amused. She also looked sexy as hell, he realised with some annoyance, in her *Medical Extremes* tank top and no make-up. She wore rain pretty well, too, he decided, remembering when he'd first met her. It seemed like months ago already.

He walked to a nearby tree and patted it, then shook it a little. It didn't move. Perfect.

'Help me with this,' he said, holding out one end of his hammock.

Her eyebrows shot up to her hairline. 'You're not serious? You're *not* sleeping in a hammock out here in the rain?'

He wrapped one end of it expertly round the tree, motioning for her to walk with her end to the next one. 'Probably not in the rain, but I like to have my spot set up.'

'But you can't sleep out here anyway, can you? What about snakes?'

'Snakes like the ground.'

'Snakes like trees, too. You're going to wrestle one for bed space, are you, Indiana Jones?'

He grinned. 'I'll be careful.'

She rolled her eyes.

'I like a quiet place to read. I might even read one of your books. Feel free to use it, too, if you need to get away. I'm afraid there's no socket for your laptop, though.'

He finished attaching the hammock to the trees, stepped back and crossed his arms, admiring his handiwork.

'Looks good, if I do say so myself. It's the best you can get. We don't mess around out here.'

Madeline was still looking at him as if he was crazy, tapping on a fallen branch with her boot. She looked away for a second, then, 'You have one of my books?'

He nodded, walking back to the hammock and sitting in it, facing her. 'Your "geopolitical thriller". It sounded interesting, and I got a good deal for it on my e-reader.'

She was blushing now.

'What's wrong?' he asked. 'Don't you want me to read it?'

'No, it's not that...'

'I felt I should know some of your work, seeing as you're here to observe mine. Fair's fair.'

He stood up. A gust of wind threw itself at the hammock and caused it to turn over on itself. More raindrops started to splatter on their skin and Ryan quickly zipped his bag up and hoisted it back over his shoulder.

'We should go. Have you seen the dining hall yet?'

'No, I've not seen anything else. The producer got called away.'

'OK—well, in that case, let me be your jungle guide, Jane.'

With his hand on the warm small of her back, Ryan guided her towards camp. On the way he noted without saying a word that his tent had been set up just one along from Madeline's, with maybe three feet between them...

The dining hall was a basic set-up, beyond the tents and makeshift toilets, which looked a lot like a giant chicken coop for humans. A wooden platform was covered only by a roof thatched with palm fronds to stop the rain getting in. Mosquito mesh stretched between wooden posts on all sides, creating walls.

He opened the mesh door, letting her step through ahead of him as she brushed the rain off her arms with her hands. Several people waved at them as they entered, but Ryan steered Madeline to where a volunteer was serving portions of white rice and boiled vegetables onto plastic plates from a huge silver pot. The boxes of bananas she'd helped to carry were stacked at either side.

'Gourmet cuisine from now on,' he said, handing her a plate.

'I don't mind rice,' Madeline said, signalling for another scoop from the kindly lady behind the table.

'You won't be saying that in three weeks' time. Better get used to these, too.'

He picked up a banana and balanced it on the side of her plate beside the rice. She didn't object.

Ryan guided her to the end of one of the long communal tables, where piles of cutlery had been dropped haphazardly into a pile in the middle. He noted Pablo and Jake in the corner, filming them as they took a seat on the bench. The rain was hammering hard on the roof again now, making a racket on the mesh. The air smelled of DEET and damp foliage and the space was filled with quiet chatter and the clanging of cutlery.

Madeline picked up a fork opposite him, and he was about to take a bite out of a piece of boiled carrot when something large and brown landed on the table—right between their plates.

Madeline screamed and jumped up from the bench. Her plate of food went flying.

Ryan jumped up, too, as everyone else started scrambling backwards. 'Tarantula,' he said, trying to sound calm.

Madeline was beside him now, and her face was a shade of white he'd rarely seen. She had both hands over her mouth, as though to muffle more screams, and was trying her best to hide behind him.

'Make that two tarantulas,' he said, peering closer at the fuzzy ball that was now untangling itself right by the condiments basket.

He felt her hand on his shoulder, clenching on his shirt.

'They nest in the thatch,' he said, pointing upwards as Jake zoomed his camera in on the hairy spiders, sitting dazed on the table where they'd fallen. 'They must have been mating and forgotten how to hold on! I'm surprised they're still alive.'

'That's one hell of a fall from grace,' someone said, and people started twittering amongst themselves again.

Ryan noticed Madeline still wasn't laughing. He also noticed tears in her eyes, and the way she was glancing at the camera, which was pointed straight at her.

'That's enough,' he said quickly, stepping forward and putting his palm over the lens.

Jake stepped backwards, his face popping out from behind the viewfinder. 'Ryan, that was *gold*!'

'She doesn't want to be on film. We discussed this, didn't we?'

'I was told to film everything.'

'Well, *I'm* telling you not to.'

He turned around, but Madeline was gone.

'Don't follow me,' he said gruffly to the cameraman. He nodded at the tarantulas, still stationary. 'And get rid of those…before their friends come looking for them.'

He marched out of the dining hall into the rain, spun around, but couldn't see her. Then he spotted a blur of white tank top heading towards her tent.

Pulling his shirt up over his head, he sprinted across the grass. The sound of frogs and cicadas was almost as loud as the rain. He watched her unzip the door hurriedly, getting it stuck halfway.

But before he could reach her he saw the two local kids who'd been sitting with Maria running up to her.

'Miss! Miss!' they were calling.

'Oh, hi,' he heard her say in surprise as he moved closer.

He watched her swiping at her face to clear away what was obviously embarrassment and tears as much as rain. One of the kids in a yellow shirt threw his arms around her waist and she stood there for a moment, seemingly unsure of what to do.

'Can we see?' he heard the boy ask, pointing to her tent.

'Curious, are you?' Ryan said, walking up to them.

The kids thought nothing of running around in the rain—they were used to it.

Madeline looked at him. The kids' arms were still locked around her.

'You can see inside,' she said kindly, untangling the

arms from around her and finishing unzipping the door. 'Actually, I have something for you.'

Madeline got to her knees and crawled to her backpack. The kids followed after her.

'Room for one more?' Ryan asked, squeezing inside. He reached for one of the boys—the one in the yellow shirt—tickling his feet until he was giggling wildly.

Madeline handed them each a colouring book, and a set of pencils between them. They looked elated.

Ryan was touched. He leaned on one elbow on the groundsheet beside her. 'You OK?'

She lifted her swollen eyes to the canvas ceiling, let out a long sigh and watched the kids roll onto their tummies and start to colour. 'He got all that on camera. I almost made a tree fall down with that scream.'

'He won't use it.'

'How do you know?'

'I told him not to.'

She met his eyes, and mouthed *Thank you* over the kids' heads.

The little boy looked up. 'Why you cry, miss?' he asked.

Madeline put a hand out to touch his damp hair. 'I saw something scary,' she said.

'A tarantula,' Ryan followed up.

The boy beamed, showing gappy teeth. 'Tarantula not scary.'

'To me they are,' Madeline said. She looked at Ryan, 'Especially when they fall an inch from your dinner plate.'

The kid put his pencil down, got to his feet and pulled his friend up. *'Vamos!'*

'What?' Madeline laughed now.

'Vamos!'

She got to her feet, followed him outside, and Ryan went with them. The light was fading fast but he had a vague idea what the boys were going to show her.

They took her hands, one on either side of her, and led her to the same area where he'd strung up his hammock. The rain was still falling, but covered by the trees it was less noticeable.

They pulled Madeline to a thick tree trunk and dropped her hands, busying themselves walking around the tree, peering at it closely.

'Home!' one of them exclaimed after a moment. 'Look!'

Ryan put a hand to Madeline's elbow gently, throwing her a warning look. She frowned and turned to where they were pointing, then walked as close as she could to the tree and peered into a hole in the bark.

'Wow!' She stepped backwards, then seemed to compose herself.

The kids were giggling again, pointing to another hole in the bark. 'Spider house!' The youngest one giggled, tugging on her shirt.

Each hole in the tree was indeed a house. Ryan knew it well. Nestled inside each cosy mossy crevice was a giant tarantula, just waiting for nightfall.

'They come out when it's dark and hang out on the tree,' he explained.

Madeline scrunched her face up just long enough for him to note her disdain, but he admired how she tried to look excited for the boys.

'Wow, that's great,' she said.

'They're not so scary when you see them like this, are they?' Ryan replied.

He couldn't help the smile stretching out his face.

CHAPTER EIGHT

MADELINE DISAGREED. THEY were tarantulas. They were terrifying wherever they were—not that she wanted to make even more of a fool of herself than she already had. She half expected the kids to reach into the holes and grab a few, start stroking them like cuddly toys just to prove a point.

She backed away and was surprised when Ryan held his shirt above their heads to shelter them both as he led them back to their tents.

'Probably should have brought an umbrella,' he said, catching her glance.

She smiled at the gentleman emerging in him now, with the more time they spent together, and walked close to him, letting the kids back into her tent with her to collect their colouring books and promising she would see them again tomorrow. Then she watched them scurry off into the jungle as Ryan took their place in the tiny space.

'Amazing,' she said wistfully, aware that he was filling up pretty much every inch of spare room in her tent; it was a thin canvas bubble for the two of them. His shirt was wet, as was hers, and the sound of the rain on the canvas was louder now than ever. 'The kids, I mean.'

'They're pretty amazing, yes,' he said, leaning on one arm and stretching out.

His feet were almost touching the door. He looked as though he was making himself comfortable…as though he had no intention of leaving just yet. Madeline hadn't laid out her bed sheets yet—which she was now pretty glad about. Otherwise he would literally be lying on her bed alongside her. The thought made her nervous.

'Extremely resilient. They literally have no fear. Sometimes gets them in trouble, though.'

'I can imagine.' She swallowed.

'It was great of you to bring the colouring books. You're going to be pretty popular round here if you're planning on pulling moves like that.'

'I bought a few in Rio.' She reached for her pack and pulled out her notebook. She didn't want to admit— even to herself—how she'd frozen the moment that little kid's arms had wrapped around her. All she'd seen was Toby. But she couldn't think about Toby now. She couldn't think about his little arms around her on the ward at the hospital, his big brown eyes, the look on his mother's face when…

She took a deep breath. While Ryan was here she was determined to get some more answers from him. She was pretty up to speed on his youth now, but the closer they got to the present day, the more he seemed to skate awkwardly around her questions. She'd warm him up, she decided, by asking him something easy.

But he was looking at her quizzically. 'What's wrong?' he asked.

'Nothing,' she said, too quickly. I was just thinking… about the spiders. Being on camera looking like an idiot.'

'I told you—they won't use the footage. What else is on your mind?'

She looked at him and shrugged, flummoxed. How could he tell she had been thinking about more than the spiders? Was it because he could read the pain in her eyes the way she could sometimes read it in his?

'Nothing. So—I'm guessing you're a bit better prepared for this kind of adventure than me. What do you bring with you in your pack? Aside from the usual equipment and your hammock, I mean? You must need a different kit wherever you go…mountains, desert, jungle…'

She watched him stroke a hand across his chin, then take his hat off. He was literally three inches from her damp skin, and in the silence the symphony of crickets, frogs and raindrops seemed to rush through her like another pulse. Everything around them and between them was alive.

'You're right—it's different every time. But some things stay the same. I never go anywhere without my multi-tool.'

'What's that?' she asked, scribbling it down.

'Only the manliest tool in the world!' He reached into one of his pockets and pulled out something that looked like a penknife, flipped out one of the blades. 'It has a million features—the manufacturers sponsored Season Two of the show, didn't you see that?'

'I wasn't watching it for the sponsors.'

She could hear the smile in his voice when he carried on with his answer. 'And I carry anti-venom, of course.'

'Of course,' she said. 'Over one hundred thousand people die every year from snakebites. I saw that on one of your shows, I think.'

'Impressive memory. Wait one second.'

He crawled back out of the tent, and seconds later crawled back in again holding another fabric case. He opened it, revealing a vial and two long, plastic tubes.

'I always keep these around. Hope to God I never

need them, but you should know how to use this kit if you don't already.'

'That's OK. I'm sure plenty of people here know how to use it,' she said, eyeing the tubes warily.

'You're right, but still… We have anti-venom for most snakes out here. Simple to use—just get as much info as possible about what bit, then inject the right anti-venom into the elbow crease right here.'

He squeezed her in the spot he'd indicated, gently, making her pulse quicken again.

'You've done that before, I'm sure.'

'Yes, but like I've already said I'm not here to—'

'I'm sure you wouldn't worry too much about making excuses if someone urgently needed your help.' He put the vial and tubes down and rested on his elbow next to her. 'You haven't so far, at least.'

She bit her tongue.

'I also have a fire stick and a sharpener somewhere—oh, and we all get given a sat phone push-to-talk in case we ever get separated. I have a roll of gaffer tape, too—you never know when you'll need that—and a water purifier. Someone usually has rice and a stove in their pack in case we have to stray from camp—takes no time to use, plus it's light.'

'You're literally prepared for everything?'

He nodded. 'Have to be. Here in the jungle, though, a good knife and my British army boots are compulsory.' He motioned to the heavy black boots on his feet. 'These are something you Brits do very well. Oh, and my hammock. Naturally.'

'Everything but an umbrella,' she teased.

'And the kitchen sink.'

'Ryan…'

She put her pen down, sat cross-legged and faced him.

He was playing with his penknife now, flipping things open and closed absent-mindedly...the bottle-opener, the wire-cutter. She felt as if the tent was closing in—as though a flame had just been lit inside...one that could at any moment become a fire.

She took another breath. Then she let the question slide off her tongue. 'What's the most dangerous situation you've ever been in?'

She knew it was brave. Reckless, even. She just had to see what he'd say.

He flipped the knife blade out and in again, loudly, looking as though he was mulling the question over in his mind. 'Most dangerous?'

'Yes.'

He smirked. 'Being in the middle of the Amazon with amorous tarantulas falling from ceilings isn't dangerous enough for you?'

'I've seen you deal with worse,' she said, feeling her heart thumping against her damp clothes.

'Well, there was the pair of hikers we had to treat for hypothermia when they went off track in Iceland. Almost got screwed ourselves when the helicopter dropped us down on the winch and couldn't lift us out again because of the wind.'

'I saw that one,' she said. 'What about...?' She paused, wondering how best to phrase it—how far she could push it. She was treading on eggshells now. 'What about off-camera? Has there ever been anything so dangerous that you weren't allowed to broadcast it on television? Or talk about it afterwards?'

Ryan snapped the blade on his penknife closed one final time, then shoved it into his pocket. His icy eyes looked dark when he met hers.

He got to his knees. 'We show everything that happens, Madeline.'

'Except when *you* say not to, right?'

'What do you mean?'

'Like when women scream over falling spiders?'

He narrowed his eyes. 'The producers and editors have the final say.'

'Except when *you're* adamant that something isn't shown. Am I right?'

'I knew this was a mistake.'

He turned from her, started unzipping the tent, his fingers an angry blur. Madeline got on all fours and crawled closer to the door.

'Where are you going?'

'To my tent. We're done here.'

'What just happened?'

Ryan moved to step out, but turned at the last minute, bringing his face right up to hers. The trees were swaying behind him and the wind rushed in with the rain, making her shiver in spite of the heat.

'I told you we'd start at the beginning,' he growled.

'That's what we're *doing*!'

She'd blown it. She felt as if she was talking to a completely different person.

'I don't appreciate this hidden agenda. I know what you really want to ask me, Madeline, and I don't want to talk about it.'

Her insides were twisting more and more by the second at his anger and at his words, thick and cold like ancient lava.

She forced her face to stay neutral and mirrored his stance, sitting on her haunches. 'I'm sorry,' she said. 'But I'm writing your memoir, Ryan. You have to at least appreciate that your publishers are asking me questions about what happened that day…what you don't want anyone to know…'

'They're asking you to call me out. They want *you* to prove that the perfect, selfless hero you see on the television isn't real… They want it from the horse's mouth, don't they? So the world can get a kick out of how the mighty fall.'

Madeline was stunned. 'What? Why would anyone do that?'

'You tell me.'

'I would never write anything to hurt you or compromise your integrity.'

'We both know that's what they want so they can get more sales!'

'That doesn't mean we can't write it properly—say what *you* want to say…'

'Damn it, Maddy, I don't want to say anything at all!'

His hand was still on the tent's doorway and she watched helplessly as he unzipped the rest of it roughly and crawled out.

'Wait, Ryan—can we just talk about this?' she pleaded, sticking her head out into the rain after him.

But he was walking through the expanding puddles of mud, back towards the dining hall. She looked at the vial of anti-snake venom in its pack, still on the floor. Through the rain now striking viciously at everything in its path, Madeline could barely even see Ryan any more.

CHAPTER NINE

THE JUNGLE, RYAN thought from his place in the hammock, was merely a microcosm of the world in its entirety—a giant muddle of monsters trying not to look as if they'd eat you alive if they had to.

He sipped his coffee from the warm metal mug and thought that this might be something he'd tell Madeline for the memoir—after all, he'd seen a lot of the world, battled to save many of those harmed by the monsters in it.

But then he remembered with a small sigh that he was going to steer clear of Madeline for a while.

He'd seen her at breakfast, talking to Evan, who was just back from the hospital in Manaus with good news, thankfully. She'd glanced up and their eyes had met over the dining bench. He swore he'd seen her hand rise in cautious greeting, but he'd turned from her, grabbed his caffeine fix and some fruit and headed straight here.

He didn't want to make small talk and he damn well wasn't going to apologise to her either; he wasn't going to do *anything* with the cameras lurking like jaguars waiting to pounce.

'Ryan!'

A voice calling his name almost made him spill his

coffee. He sprung up from the hammock as Maria came into view, wearing her *Medical Extremes* uniform.

'Sorry to interrupt, but could we have your assistance?'

He was already walking towards her, annoyed with himself for hiding away too long. 'Of course, I was just finishing up. What's happened?'

'Skin condition and a fever with it. Evan and the other guys went back to the landing pad for the rest of the supplies.'

'I'm on it,' he said, walking faster with her towards the stations, kicking himself internally.

If he hadn't left the dining hall when discussions about fetching more supplies were underway he'd have known to be there already. Annoyance made his brow crease— Madeline was already affecting his work. All the more reason to stay away from her.

When they reached the medical stations bright sunlight was streaming into the clearing and a line of people had gathered, waiting to register. Three volunteers were taking their details, all of them in their trademark *Medical Extremes* T-shirts and hats. The rain had cleared in the night, and there were only a few fast-evaporating puddles to show for its appearance.

Madeline was talking to a small group of kids who'd gathered around her in a corner of the camp. Sunshine danced in her long hair. She was wearing a white tank and khaki shorts, exposing long, milky legs, and she was handing out the rest of the colouring books and pencils. Her eyes caught his as he passed her and he tried not to flinch visibly.

She was doing something good, of course, and having her do something practical around camp was better than her scribbling reams of notes about his shady past. But the sight of her caused something in his stomach to shift.

For a moment she looked as though she was going to say something, but he tore his eyes away before she had the chance, followed Maria into one of the medical stations and flipped the switch in his mind he always flipped when it came to focussing entirely on a patient in his care.

'What seems to be the problem here?' he asked as he approached a guy lying flat on one of the makeshift beds.

He was bare-chested, wearing faded red shorts down to his knees, probably in his mid to late thirties. His forehead was clammier than it should be, even in this thick heat, and several raised lesions on his legs and arms showed clear lines of demarcation at the edges.

Erysipelas lesions, he noted. It was a bacterial infection, common in these parts—simple to treat but dangerous if left too long.

He walked to the airtight container in the corner of the station, aware now of Jake in the other corner, filming him. He pulled out one of the kits inside as Maria translated the man's answers from his quick Spanish. He'd been feeling ill for two days, with headaches and vomiting, but had tried to push on without telling anyone. The muddy splashes on his legs showed he must have walked at least some way through thick jungle to get to them.

'We'll soon have this under control,' Ryan said, pulling on a pair of gloves and getting out the antihistamine. He'd have to be given prophylactic antibiotics, too.

He was explaining what his patient would have to do to ensure the lesions healed properly when a whirlwind seemed to sweep into the station. He turned and saw a little girl with braids in her long hair, no older than four or five, waving her arms around, bolting towards them.

'Daddy!' she shouted, reaching them in a flash and placing her little hands on the side of the bed.

Her cheeks were streaked with tears and her pale blue dress was covered in mud. His patient reached for her hand and started comforting her with soothing words in spite of his obvious torment. Ryan's heart broke a little.

Two seconds later someone else entered the station. Madeline.

'There you are,' she said to the little girl, walking over to her and placing a hand gently on her shoulder. 'Come on, they're treating your daddy and we have to let them work.'

She swept a hand through her own hair and Ryan was thrown for a moment—not least by the sight of her standing beside him. She switched to Spanish and, he assumed, repeated what she'd just said. The little girl gripped her hand.

This time he let his eyes linger on Madeline's as he pulled the packaging away from the hydrocortisone. He tried to ignore the rush of adrenaline he felt tearing through him as her sea-green gaze seemed to rip straight down the wall he'd been building around himself after their somewhat heated debate.

She stood there talking to the girl and ignoring *him* as he cleaned the man's wounds and bandaged the worst one, then made him promise to take it easy for a few days while the antibiotics did their work.

As he and Maria worked Ryan was aware of Madeline heading to the corner with the child, away from the camera, making her laugh, making her tears all but disappear. He wished he could hear and understand more of what she was saying.

By the time his patient was walking towards his daughter to receive a welcoming hug Madeline seemed to have become firm friends with her. Ryan tried not to give the impression that he'd noticed, but a part of him was more impressed with her than ever. What the hell had made her quit nursing? She obviously had a way with people—especially children. And hadn't she at one point during their extensive chats told him that she'd worked at St David's in London? The children's hospital? That must have been where she'd honed her skills at earning their trust.

He watched her step outside—saw the way she immediately became swarmed over by the kids. He was about to follow but another patient was being brought inside, this time by Mark. As the makeshift plastic sheet that served as a doorway fell down after him he heard her telling them all to follow her to the shade—that much he understood in Spanish.

'She's pretty good with those kids,' Mark said, sitting the patient—a lady in her mid-twenties—down on the chair beside the now empty bed.

'Who? Madeline?' Ryan said nonchalantly, stripping the paper from the bed and shoving it into a plastic bag.

'Yes, of *course* Madeline! She's got them all colouring under the trees out there like friggin' Mary Poppins. Usually they're running around under our feet by now and asking to wear the stethoscopes. Impressive Spanish, too. Did you know she was fluent in that as well as Portuguese? I think she said she lived in Colombia for a while.'

'Yes.'

Maria stifled a smile as she marked their last patient's notes on a clipboard.

'She's quite a hit out there,' Mark continued, oblivious to Ryan's curt tone. 'I hope you don't mind, but I told her she could make a start on the dental hygiene project if she wanted something to do. Gave her the toothbrushes and worksheets. I figured Evan would have done the same thing. I know you guys are working on the memoir together, but—'

'The more hands on deck the better,' Ryan cut in, before the questions and the digging could start.

He had a feeling the team had all talked about the damn memoir behind his back already, and it made him uncomfortable to say the least. He caught Maria's sideways glance as he took his new patient's blood pressure.

'Everything OK?' she asked.

'Fine.'

He reached for a bottle of water. It was barely nine a.m. and already hotter than hell. The rain hadn't cooled things off for long, and there was undoubtedly more on the way. More patients, too.

It was several hours before he stuck his head outside into the sunshine. Evan and the others had fetched more antibiotics and yet more boxes of fruit. There was talk of a swim in the waterfall that he registered vaguely before Madeline caught his attention again.

He swigged from his water bottle, then stretched out his muscles, battling the urge to walk over to her. He'd been on form—performing routine duties one after the other, talking to the camera, trying not to let her creep into his thoughts. He was tired, he realised. And their argument was bothering him again.

From where he stood she seemed to be fully absorbed in what the children were doing, and he noticed that someone had stacked several cardboard boxes on the plastic sheets they were sitting on. She was laughing and smiling in the sunshine, her skin glistening with sunscreen and probably DEET. Maybe both.

He wandered over to her. Shutting her out was even more exhausting than letting her in.

'Colombia?' he said, clearing his throat, leaning on a nearby tree. 'You lived there for two years on and off? Is that right?'

The wind ruffled her loose hair, and from his stance looking down at her sitting cross-legged on the ground he could see her bra and the way it hugged her breasts beneath her tank top. He tried not to look as she fixed her gaze on him.

'Well remembered. Medellin, then Cartagena.'

A yellow and brown butterfly fluttered between them.

'I was writing a book.'

'Another geopolitical thriller?' he asked, folding his arms.

'A romance, actually.'

Her tone was blunt, and for the first time he considered that perhaps she was angry with him for what had happened yesterday. He *had* kind of turned on her out of the blue. Not that she hadn't deserved it after prying where she wasn't invited.

'It didn't really go anywhere. Guess I'm not too great with romance.'

He frowned, swallowed an apology before it bubbled out of him—she *had* to know there were lines she couldn't cross. And more that *he* couldn't cross, he added to himself.

'So, how do you feel about being involved in this?' he asked, gesturing to the dental hygiene boxes around them and the paper she had already handed out to the kids along with the colouring books.

'I think it's a great idea.' She got to her feet and faced him. 'Was it one of yours?'

'Actually, it was Maria's. It was kind of a joint wish for all of us to promote healthy eating, dental hygiene, basic first aid…all that as we go along. You start with the kids and it filters through to the elders, you know? How are those mosquito bites?'

He pointed to one on her arm—a small red welt. She covered it with her hand. 'I'll survive. Anyway, I think this is a good thing to be involved in. Teaching them basic health education while you're playing games—they think it's all fun.'

'Exactly. We wanted to focus first on helping them learn about brushing their teeth.'

Madeline nodded, looking at the fact sheets in Spanish about exactly that. Ryan noted one of the boxes was open, so she'd clearly seen the six hundred toothbrushes they'd brought with them.

'I've been colouring, then stopping to talk through the fact sheets, then colouring again…'

'Good start. And if you want to add songs at any point they love that.'

'Songs?'

'Evan plays guitar sometimes—makes up words. How are you at improvising?'

She shrugged. 'I guess I could give it a shot.'

Once again he was impressed. Having another pair of hands on the project would be a blessing. In other places where they'd tested the programme they had already seen an improvement in dental health and knowledge about how to prevent parasite infestation. It was one of their success stories, but they still had so much more to do.

Madeline shifted her weight from one foot to the other. 'Listen, Ryan, about last night…'

'It's forgotten,' he said quickly.

She let out a sigh. 'No, it's not, I can tell.'

He took her elbow, led her three steps away from the kids and lowered his voice. His hand tingled, just feeling her skin against his, and he withdrew it quickly, slightly shocked.

'Like I said, there are things I don't want to talk about, Madeline. *Ever.* I know you have a job to do, but if we could leave certain things out I'd appreciate it.'

'It's not going to work like that,' she said, frowning at him. 'You know the publishers will want answers about Josephine.'

A planet-sized rock shot up to his throat. Her name... *her* name...coming from Madeline's lips sent chills straight through him.

'We can write around it, but the stories...or the half-stories...are out there already.'

She reached for his arm. That spark again. He had to take a step back. His fists balled of their own accord.

'We can work this out,' she hurried on in a hushed tone, closing the gap again. 'You *have* to trust me, Ryan. Just trust me with the truth.'

Another butterfly caught on the wind beside her as he ran his eyes over her lips, her ears, the apple dangling on a chain around her neck. He wanted to trust her. He really did. She had some kind of strange effect on him... And maybe it was finally time for the truth.

He considered it for a second. Josephine and the real story behind that day had turned him into a walking wreck for the most part—shot a bullet through any real chance of a romance ever since. They'd all wanted to know what had happened and he'd flat out refused to say, building a wall up brick by damn brick till it was suffocating for all involved. Maybe it *was* time.

He opened his mouth, but one of the kids—a girl in a muddied shirt—jumped up and screeched with laughter, dragging a little boy with her over to Madeline. They both started talking to her excitedly in fast Spanish, pulling at her hands.

He closed his mouth.

'Sorry—you were saying?' Madeline said after a moment, breaking free.

The look of expectancy in her eyes tore him to pieces. He bit his cheeks. What the hell was he thinking? It wasn't time. It would never be time. He was letting his unnamed emotion and the heat interfere with his mental processes and it could never happen again.

'I don't trust anyone,' he said quickly, before his heart could hold him back.

He'd expected anger, and prepared himself to take the hit, but instead he watched confusion flood Madeline's eyes, then perhaps a hint of pity.

'That's a shame,' she replied softly. 'You must be really lonely.'

Then she sat down again with the kids, leaving him speechless.

CHAPTER TEN

MADELINE SAT ON the edge of the lake, drawing circles in the murky water with her bare feet. She clutched her coffee cup, turned the page of the book she was reading, but the words weren't sinking in.

She sighed, putting it down on the wooden deck, watching the dragonflies skimming the surface and leaving tiny ripples in their wake. One week in and she was growing to know each creature that dared to show itself around the camp—thanks to a book Maria had leant her.

She knew the iridescent *Rhetus periander* butterflies, with their vivid blue wings and red blotches, the black grasshoppers with their beady indigo eyes and bright yellow polka dots, the russet-coloured caterpillars which clung resiliently to leaves throughout every rainstorm and the sand flies that nibbled in invisible silence at her legs and feet, leaving marks she needed to remind herself constantly not to scratch.

Madeline knew a lot about her new surroundings already. But she still didn't know enough about Ryan.

Time passed slowly in the jungle. In seven days she hadn't once looked at herself in a mirror, but she could tell she'd lost weight. Her shorts were loose on her, as were her dresses. Even her bikini, which she was wearing now, wasn't as figure-hugging as it had been when she'd bought it. Rice and fruit were now the essentials to stop a rumbling stomach rather than something to enjoy.

Her phone had died three days ago. When Evan had offered her the solar charging kit she'd told him she didn't need it, instead charging her Dictaphone for yet another interview with Ryan that she knew wouldn't go anywhere.

In every awkward chat since that day under the tree he'd refused to step any closer towards the place she needed him to be—and that was the place where Josephine came into the picture.

She furrowed her brow at the shimmering water ahead. Madeline would only get paid if she delivered the kind of manuscript the editor had in mind. She was trying not to feel defeated but she couldn't really help it.

She couldn't help the chemistry still more than evident between her and Ryan either. Even thoughts of Jason were dwindling by the day. Their break-up had been a meteoric crash in her world, but she felt so far away from that now. Since coming out here she'd been swept into another existence entirely—one in which she was perpetually hot, sticky and dancing in dangerous circles around Ryan.

She shivered, even in the heat, remembering the night before.

Ryan had agreed to another interview on the condition that she accompany him fishing. Mark and Evan often went out on the river at night, and she'd been once, just for the boat ride and to clear her head. She'd never been off camp with Ryan. When he'd asked her to join him she'd been surprised, nervous and grateful all at the same time, because he'd chosen to spend most nights alone up till then, preparing equipment, stock-checking, talking to the camera or just hiding himself away in his tent.

She shivered again, twirling the water with her toes as her mind replayed what had happened in the boat.

'Ever tasted a piranha?' Ryan had asked, casting his line out into the blackness of the water.

The moon had been a bright yellow bulb above them, and with no other lights they'd been able to see a million stars. They'd also heard bats and monkeys in the treetops as they'd discussed his training days and a family vacation to the UK for the memoir.

Madeline had felt the Amazon closing in on them as he'd rowed them further away from camp. She'd sensed a thousand eyes and ears around them in the darkness— furry spies, she'd hoped, as opposed to any kind of drug runner.

She'd gripped the side of the small boat, watching his profile and keeping an eye out for caimans. 'Never,' she'd replied in answer to his question. 'What do they taste like?'

'A lot like sardines. They're pretty good when they're crunchy off the grill, but they're bony little things. Kind of a mission to get the meat off. Here—hold this.'

He'd thrust the fishing line at her then, and reached behind him to the small box he'd brought along and shone a flashlight into it. She'd seen raw chicken.

'They go crazy for this,' he'd told her, reaching for the line again.

His hand had brushed hers and he'd stood just an inch behind her, hooking tiny chunks of the white meat onto the end of the wire. She hadn't wanted to ask why *they* weren't being fed this luxury.

'Now, throw it in.'

'Me?' she'd asked, still processing the jolt she'd felt at his touch.

'This is a good spot. Don't panic—you'll be OK.'

He'd put the line back in her hands and moved up close behind her. Very close. So close that she'd felt his breath tingling over the nape of her neck below her ponytail. He'd put his hands over hers and lifted the line, helping her throw it into the water—hard.

Nothing.

Then everything.

The water had started moving around the end of the line.

'There they are!' Ryan had exclaimed excitedly, shining his light out ahead of them and putting a hand on her shoulder, over her clammy skin.

Madeline had gasped, feeling her face break out into a grin as a white-topped frenzy came into view. It had been as though someone had installed a tiny hot-tub in the middle of the river.

She'd felt the line tug as Ryan rested his flashlight on the bench, facing them.

'Don't let go—pull it in! Don't let the line go loose,' he'd urged as his hands moved to her quickly, gripping her waist over her thin blue dress to hold her steady.

'Don't let go of *me*—they'll eat me, too,' she'd said, leaning further into him.

'I won't. You've got it—you've got it...'

He'd been pressed against her in the boat. His head almost resting on her shoulder from behind as he'd helped her pull the fish in through the frenzy and over the side.

'Great job!' he'd cried, elated, holding up the line and moving away from her to reach for the flashlight again.

He'd shone it on their catch—a silvery fish about twice the size of a goldfish, with an orange tinge. It hadn't looked very scary, even as it wriggled and flapped. Madeline had reached for the line to get a closer look but Ryan had gripped her fingers and held them tight away from it.

'Not so fast!'

'Sorry.'

'You want to see what this thing will do if it gets a hold of your finger?'

His face had been so close to hers she'd practically been able to feel his stubble tickling her cheek. She'd smelled him: a raw, animal scent mixed with sunscreen that had made her a little wobbly on her feet. Luckily she'd been able to blame the boat for that.

He'd stuck a hand in his pocket, pulled out a thick green leaf. Holding the line with the fish still attached, he'd dangled the leaf in front of the piranha. Instantly the fish had opened its jaws, revealing an ominous row of razor-sharp teeth, and started chomping the leaf to pieces from bottom to top with ferocious zeal, as fast and as efficient as a chef's knife chopping a cucumber.

Madeline had watched with equal amazement and horror.

'Told you—you don't want to mess with these guys.'

Ryan had grinned, turned off the light and thrown what was left of the leaf overboard. His eyes had sparkled like ice cubes in the moonlight, and Madeline had sworn she'd never seen anyone so handsome in her entire life as Ryan when he was smiling, living in the *now*, not letting his past weigh him down like a hunk of lead.

'That's the most incredible thing I've ever seen,' she'd breathed, laughing with the sheer adrenaline of it.

She'd studied his lips, his mouth—so different from Jason's. She'd been so certain that she'd never even want to kiss someone else. But in that moment, awed by their primitive environment and slightly scared of the flesh-eating fish, she'd known she'd say *To hell with professionalism* and kiss Ryan Tobias if he'd initiated it.

As his eyes had raked over her lips under the infinite

Milky Way she'd willed him to throw her down in that rickety boat and erase every last trace of her ex, and the others before him, from out of her for ever. At one point she'd been convinced he was going to—because Madeline had seen it in Ryan, too—looked it straight in the face.

That hunger. That unmistakable desire.

But he'd tossed the fish into the box under the chicken and rowed them back to camp in silence. Then, instead of sitting around the fire with her and the others, he'd given the piranha to Evan to roast, retreated to his tent alone and hadn't even said goodnight...

The trees shifted behind her, signalling that her time alone at the camp's only washing facility was almost up.

Madeline put her cup down by her book and jumped into the water with the small bar of organic soap she'd been given. It was one that left no trace of any chemicals behind. She swam for a few metres under the surface, popped her head up and looked back.

Her heart leapt like a rabbit as she saw Ryan standing on the deck, peeling off his shirt.

Had he seen her?

Her eyes glued themselves to his body. His muscles were rippling in the early-morning light; his unshaven face was shadowed around his jaw. He was fiddling with the button on his khaki trousers now, undoing it, sliding the trousers down his strong, lean legs and shrugging them off.

Madeline froze. If she moved he would see her. She considered closing her eyes, but it was too late. His boxers were already halfway down his legs and he was kicking them aside with his trousers and towel.

He was going for a swim. *Naked.*

Her breath caught in her throat. He lifted his arms

and stretched up to the sun, as though expecting Mother Nature herself to stand and applaud her own fine work of art. Perhaps she was. The wind was riffling through the trees around the little lake, causing the cicadas to up the volume of their hum.

Madeline swallowed, digging her feet into the squelchy mud below her. She'd never seen a man with a body like his before. Ryan Tobias was pretty much perfect—the quintessential 'hot doc' calendar contender for the month of August, standing like some idolised enigma in shafts of yellow sunlight.

Bending over in the sunlight.

Pointing his hands at the water in the sunlight.

He dived in.

Madeline panicked.

She traced the line he was leaving on the surface with her eyes, as though he himself were a pack of piranhas. She considered swimming past him at full throttle and clambering out before he had the chance to see her. But, again, she was too late.

The water rippled out in front of her and his head appeared. Then his eyes sprang open, looking right into hers from less than a foot away.

'Hi,' she said, under her breath.

He shook his hair, sending a shower of droplets out around him. 'Good morning.'

'Didn't you see my book on the deck, with my cup?'

Her toes were still curling into the mud under the water. She couldn't see her feet, or anything else—a fact she was glad of as he stood there with a look of amusement spreading from his cool grey eyes down to his twitching lips.

He's naked, she couldn't help reminding herself, feeling the colour rise to her cheeks.

'Nope—didn't see. I was half asleep till I jumped in here. We had an emergency in the night so I didn't get much sleep.' He stepped closer to her, spreading his arms out on either side as though trying to gather the water between them. 'Nice surprise.'

Naked, naked, naked.

'What was the emergency?' she asked, stepping backwards slightly, aware that if she stayed where she was she might accidentally touch him with a very inappropriate part of her body.

'Poisonous caterpillar got to one of the kids and his finger swelled up so much the poor thing had a blue hand.'

He stopped right in front of her, his bare torso inches from her breasts in her purple bikini. She studied his face in the sun—the bronzed cheeks, the faint lines around his eyes—noticed how his eyelashes caught drops of water from his dripping hair before he blinked and set them on their downward path again.

Madeline felt as if she was under a searchlight all of a sudden, and another memory from the night before, of his hands on her waist in the boat, flooded her mind and her loins at the same time.

She turned onto her back in the water and felt his eyes on her breasts as they stuck above the surface like her toes. She studied the swaying branches overhead, and the darting dragonflies, reminding herself to breathe.

'Is the kid OK?' she asked without looking at him.

He floated on his back beside her. 'Yes, he's good now. Morphine always helps.'

'You must be exhausted.'

'All in a day's work. Or a night's. And I'm not the only one working hard—how's it going with your group of kids? You seem to really love them, and we can all see how much they love *you*.'

Madeline closed her eyes, swallowing as his fingers brushed hers under the water. She was still clutching her organic soap and he took it out of her hand gently, stood upright and then, to her surprise, took her left foot gently in his hands and ran the soap over it while she floated.

This was definitely not happening. Ryan was not going out of his way to touch her.

'I do,' she said in reply to his statement, though the words came out a little strangled. 'Love the kids, I mean.'

She tilted her head to look at him, but he seemed to be willing her not to say a word about what he was doing. In silence he trailed the soap between each and every one of her toes and massaged them with firm fingers... slowly, sensually.

Madeline's insides were on fire. Ryan wouldn't let her stand, though. He kept her feet against him, pulling her soles to his solid chest as he continued his massage, then worked the soap up her legs softly, firmly, then softer again.

If she hadn't been lying in a lake she'd be wet for other reasons by now, she realised, groaning inwardly.

'I don't know why you gave up nursing, Maddy,' he said softly, breaking into her thoughts.

He let her feet go but moved to her side, placing one hand under her back. He started to trail the soap softly in a circle around her navel.

'We've spoken about me a lot, but why don't we talk about *you*?'

Madeline was struggling to maintain an air of calm, and she somehow levelled her voice, closed her eyes and allowed him to wash her. No one had ever done anything like this to her before.

'There's nothing to say. I'm happy to leave all that stuff to you guys while I write.'

He ran the soap between her ribs, up to the string at the front of her bikini. He pressed it against her flesh, released it and slowly ran the soapy trail up, up, *up* over her collarbone and neck. Then, with nimble fingers, he moved the hand that was beneath her in the water to the back of her bikini top and pulled it undone.

Every part of her was throbbing with desire.

'Is this what they call a medical extreme?' she whispered daringly as he pulled the flimsy fabric from her body, leaving her top half exposed to the sun and the sky.

She thought she caught a smile on his face. He trailed the soap over her nipples, taking his time, seemingly relishing the equal amounts of thrill and torture he was causing her. She could still sense his silent urging for her not to mention what was happening, just to let him continue. It was the most erotic situation she'd ever been a part of.

His body towered over hers, blocked the sun, and from behind her eyelids she could see him taking her in. She could feel his own longing mounting by the millisecond as he trailed the soap down over her midriff, down, down to her bikini bottoms.

'My God, you're beautiful,' she heard him say hoarsely.

She couldn't take it any more. She put her feet to the ground, moved her hand under the water to feel for what she had no doubt would be standing to attention like a soldier—but he grabbed her fingers, held them tight.

'Not yet.'

'Ryan...'

'Someone's coming.'

An enormous splash by the deck made her jump. She

ducked under the water up to her shoulders and Ryan thrust her bikini top into her hands beneath the murky surface, sprang away from her side. Someone was swimming out in their direction, but she couldn't make out who it was.

With trembling fingers she rushed to tie her top up and noticed Ryan swimming four feet away from her, as if nothing had happened. As if they were just two strangers in a lake.

Her insides were doing cartwheels, and so were her thoughts. *Did that just happen?* What the hell were they thinking? They were here to work...not to romp about in the jungle like two wild animals. She wasn't another one of his lovesick fan girls—she was a professional writer on an assignment. And she was too heartbroken over her ex to notice anyone else anyway...*wasn't* she?

She rolled her eyes. She wasn't any more, and she knew it.

Whoever it was who'd come for a swim wasn't from the camp, she realised. The masculine figure swam right past her and carried on. She turned back to Ryan but he wasn't there. He was already swimming back to the deck.

He was climbing out, wrapping a towel around his waist, scooping up his clothes as if he'd already forgotten she'd ever been there. Then he walked quickly back the way he'd come through the trees, leaving her alone and still trembling.

CHAPTER ELEVEN

IT WASN'T AS if he could have stopped himself, Ryan thought, buttoning up a fresh white shirt outside his tent and raking a hand through his hair as he walked quickly back towards the medical stations. His hands had moved before his head had even been able to begin to process what he was doing.

Madeline had been floating there next to him with the sun in her beautiful green eyes, wearing next to nothing, and he'd been completely naked. He was only human, for God's sake.

A stupid human.

He'd been careless, and that had been a close call.

'Ryan!'

It was Maria, calling him over to one of the stations. He strode across the grass towards her, past the line of people waiting to register for treatment. He kicked a football that flew at him from the group of children clearly waiting for Madeline and waved at them, putting on a happy face.

His heart was pounding harder by the second. What if one of the camera guys had caught sight of them just now, with a telescopic zoom and an eye for making some seriously dramatic television? Not that anyone *here* would do that, he realised thankfully, but still, nothing would stop them talking amongst themselves about him and Madeline.

He clenched his fists at his sides. He couldn't keep away from her. Even being angry with her didn't help. Madeline Savoia was a bomb threatening to detonate right in front of him, and she was all the more dangerous for the way she was sliding into his conscience, getting under his skin.

All he'd wanted to do last night in that boat was lay her down and feast on the look of wonder and excitement in her eyes as he showed her even *more* new things. Hell, the things he wanted to show her...

He loved how empathetic she was, how readily she'd adjusted to her new environment, never once complaining about how harsh and hard it was to be out here. The kids adored her and lined up for her in the mornings, bringing her fruit and flowers and any other present they could think of to make her smile. Maria was lending her books.

She was the saint of the whole damn camp already.

'Ryan,' Maria said, leading him inside. She looked agitated. 'We just had a radio call—there's a patient on the way from the village. Mark and one of the volunteers are bringing her in on the boat right now.'

'What's the problem?' he asked, glancing at another volunteer, who was wrapping a strip of gauze around a teenage boy's forearm in the chair beside him. The air was thick and hot and smelled of antiseptic spray and disinfectant. He scrubbed his hands at the basin of water.

'Seventeen-year-old girl, name Abigail, severe abdominal pains. Mark's already diagnosed her with an ectopic pregnancy, ruptured tube...'

'We have methotrexate close if we need it?' he asked, drying off his hands on a paper sheet. It was the safest and quickest way to induce abortion.

'Already on it,' Maria said, doing up her scrubs as he prepared the laparoscope. 'This kid sounds like she's been through a lot already, from what Mark says. She's been hanging out here the past two days with her little brother and Madeline—she probably didn't even know she was pregnant.'

'Madeline?' Ryan turned around, pulling on a pair of surgical gloves.

As he spoke her name the plastic sheet over the door was swept aside and Madeline came rushing in, this time beside Mark and a volunteer, followed by Jake with his camera.

The canvas stretcher they were carrying held the pregnant girl in question, and he recognised her immediately from the village. Long-haired, chatty Abigail, lying on her back with her belly exposed, letting out the most horrific howls. It wasn't clear at all that she was pregnant, but the blood on her skirt made his heart sink.

Madeline was clutching the sweaty girl's hand, talking fast in Spanish. As they brought the stretcher up to the bed he didn't miss the tears in her eyes. Her hair was still wet, tied in a bun on her head and she met his glance for half a second—a glance that said nothing but, *Help this girl*.

Ryan could see that her nursing instincts were primed once again, probably pushing all thoughts about what had just happened at the lake completely out of the window.

He was already in action. As the camera circled he helped Mark and Maria get the sobbing Abigail gently off the stretcher and onto the table. Her skin was damp, and had a greyish tinge that concerned him. A crowd of people had gathered at the opening to the medical station, but Mark walked over and ushered them all away.

Madeline looked as though she was going to leave, too,

but Abigail reached for her arm, clutched it and gripped on as if her hand was a metal vice.

'*No quiero que te vayaso,*' she was begging in Spanish. 'Don't go, please.'

'We'll have to do keyhole,' Ryan told Maria, who nodded in agreement.

'What? Here?' Madeline looked shocked.

The girl sobbed, gripping her even tighter.

'It's better than open surgery. Quicker recovery, less blood loss. Maria—general anaesthetic...'

'Yes, Doc.'

Maria turned around to the trolley that held the equipment she'd prepared the second the radio call had come in. They were lucky to have a laparoscope—a long fibre optic cable system which allowed them to see the area in question on a monitor connected to a generator, which they charged via solar power. It wouldn't cause the girl too much extra trauma.

Madeline appeared traumatised enough in this moment for everyone, but Abigail was still latching on to her like a leech.

'Crap!' Mark exclaimed from the doorway. 'Lady out here with a hip fracture—we need you, Maria.'

'Now?'

Jake was having a field-day, zooming in on their expressions, Ryan could tell.

'Evan's tied up...'

'It's urgent,' Mark told her. 'I'll meet you next door.'

'I can't!' Maria protested.

'You guys get on it. Madeline's here,' Ryan declared, reaching behind him quickly and grabbing some scrubs from a box. He threw them at Madeline.

Her eyes widened in terror. 'Ryan... Ryan, listen... I really can't do this...'

'Yes, you can—you're just helping me. Wash your hands.'

'I can't *just help* you.'

'You're a trained nurse—of course you can. Wash your hands and put those scrubs on.'

He'd made the decision on the spot. He knew she could do it. Whatever fear she'd convinced herself she had about being in a set of scrubs around an emergency was all in her head; he was sure of it.

'I need you, Madeline,' he said calmly as he prepared the cannula and reached for the girl's hand. 'Abigail needs you.'

'I don't want to do this,' she protested again, panic causing her voice to shake. 'This isn't why I'm here. I've told you this. Stop trying to—'

'If she can't do it, Ryan, she can't do it,' Maria said, flustered. Beads of sweat were glistening on her forehead and she looked exhausted.

Ryan put the cannula down. 'Madeline is going to help me,' he said firmly, in a tone that made them both fall silent. He turned to her and fixed his eyes on hers. 'I have every faith in you. You're a nurse, Madeline. You know it and *I* know it.'

Her eyes narrowed in silent defeat. She did as she was told—scrubbed her hands, let Maria tie the scrubs at the back. Then Maria squeezed her shoulder and hurried out of the station quickly with Mark, leaving them alone with the camera.

'Trust yourself,' Ryan said, as soon as they were gone.

He heard her take a deep breath, seemingly psyching herself up. He watched her place a hand on Abigail's forehead.

'I won't leave you. I'm here,' she said in Spanish, and Abigail looked relieved, smiling weakly and muttering her thanks before Ryan administered the anaesthetic into the back of her hand.

'Muscles are relaxed, breathing is depressed, eye movements slowing,' he told her after a moment, wheeling the laparoscope closer. 'I'm going to make the incision right here.' He pointed to a spot below Abigail's belly button. 'Once the tube's in you're going to pump the carbon dioxide in for me, OK? It's really simple. I'm setting it all up. You just move your hands, slow and steady, OK?'

Madeline nodded, but didn't make a sound.

He turned the monitor around and pulled his mask up over his mouth. Madeline did the same, leaving only her eyes visible. He tried not to register the fear he saw in the wide green pools—his job right now was to make her feel as much of an expert as he was, so they could help this girl as quickly as possible.

Forty-five minutes passed, with Ryan explaining everything he was doing to the camera and making his usual trademark comments—the ones that never ceased to win him thousands of tweets from touched and inspired fans, and from wannabe medical prodigies around the world.

He could almost see them already.

Who's the new staff member? New romance? #DrRyan #MedicalExtremes.

He couldn't exactly tell them to edit this scene out as he had with the tumbling tarantulas. He blocked it from his mind. Having the camera lens on them meant he couldn't talk to Madeline either—not in the way he would have done without it—but slowly, as they worked together, he watched her fears seem to drain away, until all that was left was a determined young woman doing everything she was asked to do quickly, efficiently, in a way that made him proud.

Finally, after he'd closed the incisions with neat stitches, Madeline applied the dressing without flinching and by the time Abigail came round, groggy and confused, seemed completely calm.

Madeline pulled her mask down around her neck, stroked the girl's forehead again and held her hand, letting out a sigh.

'Ahora está OK,' she whispered. 'Dr Ryan fixed you up.'

'Nurse Maddy helped, too,' he added quickly, placing a hand on Madeline's arm.

Their eyes lingered on each other's perhaps a little too long, and when he turned to the camera he didn't miss the fact that it was directed straight at them.

Abigail was speaking now—softly, woozily. He could understand some but not all of what she said, and as she continued breathily Madeline's face was a picture of concern and fresh heartbreak.

She looked up at him, translating for his benefit. 'She says she got pregnant at fifteen, too. She went into labour for three days before coming for help, and then laboured for two more days before delivery.'

'What happened?' Ryan asked, remembering what Maria had said about Abigail's difficult past.

Madeline smudged a tear as it trickled down her cheek. 'She was induced, and then told that the baby had already passed away. A doctor from another village performed surgery, like you just did, but he wasn't a professional. So awful…'

A strange part of Ryan wanted to reach for Madeline suddenly, but he kept his hands firmly at his sides. He couldn't bear the misfortune this poor young woman had endured. Abigail was still a child herself.

'She couldn't walk for three months and was taken to the hospital in Saint Elena for physiotherapy,' Madeline said, still translating. 'She didn't know she was pregnant again, but she still wants a baby.'

Sympathy and despair for Abigail, and so many others like her, passed from Madeline to him like a secret note. Madeline's emotions were as tangible and hot as the jungle air. Her openness was rubbing off on him and she'd felt so good in his hands.

So good that in spite of being swept away again into another emergency, and trying his best to maintain focus, he still couldn't shift the image of her floating topless in the lake...of himself just moments away from making a mistake.

CHAPTER TWELVE

MADELINE HAD NEVER brushed her teeth so many times in one day. In the fading light, with her view polka-dotted by fireflies, she was sitting under the trees by the unlit fire, trying to demonstrate to the eight kids sitting around her how best to reach the backs of their mouths with their new 'toys'.

They seemed to think her sticking the toothbrush in her own mouth and making funny faces was the most hilarious thing they'd ever seen. It literally never got old. But they were learning fast, eager to impress her.

Truth be told, she was glad of the distraction, because every moment she wasn't busy she was back in that lake, being tenderly, sensually washed by Ryan.

Her cheeks flamed just at remembering, and she turned her attention back to helping the youngest child, a boy of just four, navigate his way around getting the paste out of a closed tube of toothpaste.

Her morning swim that had quickly turned into a semi-naked cleansing session at the hands of the infamous Ryan Tobias had been only marginally overshadowed by the surgery she'd helped him perform on Abigail.

Madeline was still shaking from it—picturing the blood, reliving the flashbacks that had struck like thunder as she'd pulled on those scrubs and put that mask over her face. How could she have stood there at that operating table and *not* remembered in vivid detail the last time she'd tried to help a child and failed?

She'd been so angry with Ryan that she'd almost stormed out, but the look in Abigail's eyes…it had been almost unbearable. That combined with the steel grip she'd had on her hand had given Madeline no other choice but to suck it up and follow his orders.

Ryan had forced her to face her pain today—even though he had no idea at all of what had caused it in the first place.

'Madeline, Madeline!'

One little girl called Alina was showing her a set of pearly white teeth and Madeline clapped her hands, then directed her to rinse her mouth out with bottled water and spit onto the grass.

She was annoyed with herself for being distracted. A small part of her was also annoyed at being putty in Ryan's hands after the way he'd handled her in the lake, but another part—a stronger part—was impressed that he'd called her out on her fears and, as a result, had shifted something inside her, somehow.

She smiled to herself as she watched a volunteer in knee-length denim shorts walk up with sticks and cardboard for the night's fire. Now she could think of Toby. Now she could compare the look of relief and thanks her young friend and patient had so often given her with the look of Abigail, a girl she'd been able to help. And now she could see that *both* times she'd done everything she possibly could have.

'Dinner!'

Someone called out the magic word from up at the camp, causing all the kids to start scrambling up, commencing their nightly routine of hugging her one by one,

tightly. It was their cue to head back to their families and
Madeline's to collect her boring rice and beans—not that
she ever complained.

Seeing the way people lived in the Amazon, on whatever they could catch, or grow, or fetch in small supplies
from towns after days of rowing upstream, was doing
wonders for her gratitude levels in general.

'Night!' she said to the kids one by one, hugging them
in return and watching them run off giggling into the
twilight.

She was starting to forget she'd ever lived a life in
which all thoughts of kids—of being around them, in-
teracting with them—had been torture. Maybe she'd quit
nursing too soon...

Ryan came in late to the dining room. Madeline was
sitting beside Maria, finishing a second banana, when he
walked in, grabbed a plate, filled it with food and walked
back out again. He looked as though he was in a rush.
Was there another emergency?

'Did he see another tarantula?' she joked with Maria,
scanning the ceiling for a moment.

Maria smiled and shrugged, digging her fork into a
boiled egg.

Disappointment, then annoyance swirled in Madeline's belly when she realised that Ryan might well be
ignoring her after what had happened between them.

She couldn't help reliving the image of his well-en-
dowed lower half, exposed to the sun on the deck right
in front of her, the feel of his expert hands trailing the
soap around her navel and down towards... Well... A
mistake. Surely they both knew that?

She put down her banana peel, pictured having an
early night—another torturous one with Ryan in a silent tent so close to hers—but to her surprise, when she

walked outside through the usual flurry of buzzing insects trying to get to her flesh, she saw him sitting by the fire with Evan, unpacking what looked like a box.

Madeline stopped in her tracks, but Maria beckoned her forward. She was carrying two cups of tea for them in metal cups.

'Come on, honey—come and sit down. It's been a long day,' she said kindly.

Evan was playing the guitar that she remembered Ryan talking about. They each had a beer on the ground beside them.

Ryan stood up when he saw her, holding out another beer which he'd pulled from the box on the ground. 'For you,' he said, eyes twinkling.

He'd taken his hat off and his hair was sticking up crazily again, as though he'd wrestled with a bush. He looked as rugged and wild and ridiculously handsome as the first time she'd seen him on television—except that now, of course, she'd seen parts of him his regular audience never got to see.

'Thank you,' she said, taking the lukewarm bottle from him as Maria put her tea on the ground. 'I'll drink that after,' she told her, and Maria winked.

'We had it delivered especially,' said Ryan, offering Maria one. She declined. 'Figured we had a few things to celebrate.'

The light from the fire was playing in Ryan's hair, and although he looked tired he seemed relaxed, for once. He moved across the log he was sitting on so she could sit beside him.

'A *few* things to celebrate?' she said cryptically, and he raised an eyebrow in silent acknowledgement of their secret.

Madeline felt hot—and not just because of the fire

Mark was now prodding with a long stick. She noticed Ryan's Boston Red Sox T-shirt, more casual than anything she'd ever seen him in, and his jeans as he stretched out his legs and feet towards the fire. He was still in his trusted British boots.

Others joined them as they trickled over from the dining hall. She felt Ryan's eyes on her every now and then, as hot as the sparks bouncing from the burning sticks, until eventually he leaned in to whisper in her ear.

'You did good today. You made me very proud.'

She turned to him. His face was so close she almost brushed his nose with hers, and the movement sent a familiar flight of butterflies coursing through her.

'What exactly are we talking about, here?'

He smiled, brushing her ear with his nose. 'You back in scrubs.'

She rolled her eyes, but he nudged her with his elbow.

'And out of them, of course.'

Madeline tried not to smirk as she took a sip of her drink. No one was looking at them, but she was more than aware of Jake, the camera guy, lurking not far away, no doubt waiting to catch anything juicy. She'd seen him zooming in on her before.

'That was a mistake,' she whispered, wishing she didn't have to say it.

'I know,' he said, brushing her ear again—with his lips this time.

She leaned away, her limbs growing weaker. 'I should thank you for what you had me do in surgery,' she managed after a moment.

Ryan took a swig from his bottle. Evan was strumming another song now and one of the volunteers, a lady in her thirties with straight red hair, had started to sing.

'I wouldn't have asked you to do what you did,' he said, 'if I hadn't thought all along that you could.'

'Well, you have more faith in me than I do,' she said, and sighed. 'But, seriously, you really helped me today, Ryan—more than you know. You've made me think about…things.'

'Like the thing that made you quit nursing?'

'Yes, I guess so.'

'Whatever it was, Madeline, you have to let it go. It's in the past.'

'You're right,' she said, nodding. 'Maybe *you* should remember that, too? Leave some things in the past?'

Ryan looked at the floor for a moment. A faint smile crossed his mouth as he shook his head. 'So what was it? *Who* was it that made you give up?'

'A boy called Toby,' she said, letting the words leave her mouth without giving them a chance to get stuck like they usually did.

She gripped her beer bottle in both hands, started picking at the label with her too-long nails.

'He was the first patient put in my care when I qualified—we got really close, you know? I would take him books and games, and I would tell him everything would be OK. Really, he was helping me as much as I was helping him. I was nervous, I was new, and he would say the right things… Like, "You're the best nurse, Madeline. I trust you, and I'm so glad you're here."'

'Sounds like a good kid,' Ryan said, putting his empty bottle down on the ground. 'What was wrong with him?'

'Leukaemia. Chronic lymphocytic leukaemia,' she said, feeling the familiar pang. 'He was strong for months, but one night on my shift he had sudden respiratory distress and I couldn't do anything…'

She trailed off, emotions rising.

'There was nothing I could do… He went into cardiac arrest and I couldn't even call his mother in time—'

'Of course you couldn't,' Ryan cut in, putting a big hand around her shoulder on impulse.

His voice was firm, as it had been in the medical station when he'd thrown her the scrubs. He pulled her in against him.

'You couldn't have done anything.' He shuffled closer to her on the log, moved his other hand to her knee. 'Toby never blamed you, Maddy—not for anything. And it wasn't your fault.'

'I know,' she said, putting a hand over his automatically in response. 'I know that now. But I didn't want to hear that for a really long time.'

'Because you missed him. And you felt like you'd failed him when you hadn't. You made his last few months so much better, and that was a parting gift he never would have had otherwise.'

Ryan's words were making her eyes turn to hot, wet pools again, and she blinked, not wanting to make a scene.

'Sometimes you *want* to feel the pain,' he whispered, 'because you don't believe you're entitled to feel anything else. Am I right?'

She could hear his voice crack just a little bit as he continued to hold her against him. He'd never touched her in public before. She was equally moved and afraid.

'You're so right,' she whispered back.

He looked down at his boots and after a while removed his arm from around her. She half expected him to stand up and walk away from his own feelings and the cameras yet again.

'Sometimes you think you'll just wallow in it for ever,

because you don't know how else to be any more,' she murmured.

He didn't get up. Instead he pressed his hot palm against her palm and laced his fingers through her own.

'God, Maddy,' he said on an exhale, 'I know exactly how *that* feels.'

CHAPTER THIRTEEN

HE DID KNOW. Ryan knew exactly how it felt to live under a blanket of insecurity and self-doubt. It was the exact opposite of the image he portrayed to the world.

He squeezed Madeline's hand, brought it onto his lap and looked down at their tangled fingers. The truth about Josephine seemed too big and too daunting to think about most days—even to himself. And he'd grown used to the ghosts that lived inside him…grown accustomed to the haunting taunts that had left him cold, even with a camera on his smiling face and four hundred thousand Twitter fans calling him 'hot'.

Madeline knew the bare bones of what was bothering him. He wanted to tell her everything—of course he did—because for the first time in a long time he realised he actually *needed* to talk about it.

He glanced at her profile, at the firelight bouncing in her eyes as she hummed along to Evan's music. He wanted to do so much more than talk with Madeline. She'd told him what had spawned *her* deepest insecurities. Couldn't he provide her with the same intimacy?

A frown creased his brow. Letting go of the past meant letting her in, and that was still a risk. Where would it end? Where would she stop with the information he offered her? How much would she put in a book to feed the vultures? She wasn't here to feed his ego, or his desires. She was here to write the book he'd been dreading and they both knew she couldn't give it less than her best.

'Mind if I play?'

Madeline's voice broke into his warring thoughts. She was talking to Evan. Everyone's eyes were on her so she dropped his hand back into the shadows. They'd probably seen anyway, he realised. After today, though, and the fears she'd faced in surgery, he had no doubt the producer would want to interview her about her back story, and him on why he'd been so insistent that she help him. Anything to make good TV.

At least he could pass their hand-holding off as affection between colleagues who'd saved a life.

With a slight look of surprise, Evan handed the guitar over to Madeline. He folded his arms across his chest as she pulled the instrument onto her lap.

'I only know a few songs,' she said a little shyly as she cast him a sideways glance.

Her fingers were already moving over the frets, though, creating a melody. Ryan noticed Mark and Evan grinning at each other like schoolboys, clearly impressed. Madeline had agreed to try improvising some songs for the kids, but she'd never admitted to being able to play like this. There was so much he still didn't know about this woman.

'Where did you learn to play?' he said into her ear.

'Colombia. I learned a lot there,' she replied.

Then she launched into a song he recognised immediately: *Moon River*.

Chills ran through his veins in spite of the humidity and the fire. He saw Maria's mouth fall open. Madeline could *really* sing. Her voice was like hot honey trickling over him, and he couldn't keep his eyes from her face. Her skin was glowing; her whole presence was pure light.

Ryan swore in that moment that he'd never seen or heard anything quite as exquisite as Madeline Savoia in his whole life.

When she wrapped up the final verse and chorus the circle broke out into rapturous applause—and *his* clapping, he realised, was the loudest. Evan shot him a knowing look, which he chose to ignore. For this one night, he decided, he was letting go. He was not going to give a damn what anyone thought.

'Can I keep this for tomorrow?' Madeline asked Evan, holding the guitar close against her. 'Ryan said the kids love to sing—we could probably do something fun around the dental hygiene stuff.'

'By all means, please do,' Evan said, holding his hands up. 'It sounds much better in your company than mine.'

Ryan smiled. 'I'm sure there's a tune in her about toothpaste.'

He heard Evan emit a snort—probably at the stupid words that had just slipped from his mouth. He stood up, rooted around in his pockets and pulled out his flashlight. Holding it up, he motioned for Madeline to hand him the guitar.

'I'll walk you back to the dining hall with that. No room in your tent, I'm guessing.'

She stood up herself and gave him the guitar. 'I was thinking of calling it a night anyway. It's been a long day, you know.'

'I know,' he said, feeling his pulse quicken suddenly.

He had no clue where this was leading, but he knew he had to get them both away from the fire and all the prying eyes and ears.

They wished the group goodnight, and walked away into the shadows.

'You have quite a voice, you know,' he told her, shining his light into the dining room, opening the squeaky mesh door and resting the guitar on one of the benches before stepping out again and walking with Madeline towards the tents. 'I might have followed *you* around that university campus if you'd been there,' he said, 'instead of my acapella girl. She didn't even like me back.'

Madeline laughed, pushing her hands into her pockets as they walked across the grass and stopped outside her tent. 'How do you know *I* like you?'

The air was hot, even away from the fire, and Ryan couldn't help thinking that this would be the perfect night to be out on the river again. The fireflies were holding a glow-stick party in the trees around them and all he could think about was kissing her.

He turned off his flashlight, plunging them both into darkness.

'I know you like me,' he said in reply. 'You didn't exactly bat me off this morning.'

They were hovering outside her tent now. Her hands were still in her pockets. He stepped closer, reached for her arm and let his fingers slide slowly down from her elbow to the edge of one pocket till she was forced to set her hand free. He took it again in his, clasped his fingers around it, stepped even closer.

'This morning at the lake,' he said softly. 'I knew you were there the whole time.'

He could hear the smile in her voice when she responded. 'I thought about swimming past you and getting out, but I didn't.'

She was so close to him now. The crickets seemed to be serenading them. He reached for her other hand and she released it willingly, clasping it even tighter around his fingers. The tips of their shoes were touching.

Ryan leaned in closer. Their faces were an inch apart. He could feel her breath on his nose. Every bone in his body was weakening by the millisecond…except maybe one. He brushed her lips with just his shadow, but in a heartbeat Madeline was stepping backwards, swatting at something in the darkness and cursing.

'Are you OK? What happened?' He reached for her immediately in the darkness.

'Stupid mosquitoes. Just got me hard on the ankle.'

'Did you spray?'

'I forgot.'

Her hand was still in his as she scratched at her ankle with the other one, but the moment was gone—he knew it. He could feel it slipping further away into the trees.

He sighed to himself and shook his head. 'It's always the brightest lights that attract the most mosquitos,' he said, remembering a quote he'd read somewhere once.

'I'm not shining a light.' Madeline straightened up. 'And neither are you.'

He smiled. 'It's a metaphor. Your ex was a mosquito, drawn to your light. I was thinking about this earlier. Good thing you squished him.'

She stood still in the blackness. 'Very poetic. I should write that down. But he squished *me*, so to speak.'

'It's still a good thing that all the squishing went on… I think.'

'So do I. If I was still with Jason I wouldn't be here now.' Madeline paused. 'Ryan, what's happening here?' Her question was cautious, but loaded.

'I have no clue,' he replied honestly, brushing his thumb against the side of her hand slowly.

He felt her shiver…practically felt her weaken alongside him as the moment they'd lost suddenly reappeared like a huge gaping window.

'I'm here to do a job,' she said softly, almost with regret. 'And I thought we agreed this morning was a mistake.'

He leaned forward so their foreheads were touching, feeling a zip through his insides at their closeness, at what they were surely about to do.

'Maybe it was. Maybe it wasn't. You're doing your job, Maddy, and more. So am I.'

'Not properly. I can't do it properly until you give me answers. Just now you told me you know how I've been feeling. What did you mean, exactly?'

He let out an anguished groan against her forehead. 'Why do you *do* this to me?'

'You know why. Ryan, I really don't think we should confuse this…'

'Screw thinking,' he growled.

Before she could say anything else he reached for the back of her head and pressed his lips to hers.

Madeline was almost flat against him in an instant, flowing into his arms like water as he bunched up her hair. She reached for his face, kissing him back just as hard. He felt his heart contracting and expanding in his chest as she flattened her hands against him, then clutched the material of his Boston Red Sox T-shirt as though she couldn't touch enough of him in one go. She tasted of beer and excitement, and somewhere at the back of his perpetually foggy mind he felt a cloud lifting.

Their tongues started a slow dance, then a faster tango as they kissed and kissed and kissed, and he found he was losing himself, losing his own tangled mind, for the first time in a really long time.

'We should move inside,' he whispered eventually

against her lips, heart hammering, his flesh itching to touch more of hers.

Madeline's breaths were hot and heavy as her left hand reached for the button at the top of his jeans.

He motioned to the tent. 'Inside,' he said again, more urgently.

She turned around to unzip the tent, but a rustle behind them in the trees made them freeze. A flashlight appeared, pointing straight at them.

He stepped away from Madeline. 'Who's there?'

'Ryan? It's Mark. There's an emergency—we need you at the station.'

'Dammit,' he muttered, meeting Madeline's wide eyes in the flashlight as she stood up straighter. There was disappointment etched all over her face—and his, too, he was sure. Thank God Mark was standing too far away to see them clearly. 'Be right there!' he called, trying his best to sound as though he *hadn't* just spent the last five or ten minutes glued to Madeline's face.

Mark hurried off and Ryan closed the gap between them, snaking an arm around Madeline in the darkness. He kissed her again—hard and meaningfully.

'Duty calls,' he said with another groan. 'Get some sleep.'

'Will you wake me up later?' she asked suggestively.

She was sliding a hand down his chest to his jeans again. He thanked the jungle for the darkness as something started standing to attention.

Pulling her hand away, he brought her fingers to his mouth and kissed them. 'Like you've woken *me* up?' he said gruffly. 'Madeline Savoia, you are officially killing me.'

CHAPTER FOURTEEN

WITH HER HANDS against Ryan's firm torso, even with his T-shirt between her and his bare flesh, Madeline had felt rocket ships launch inside her.

She rolled over in her sleeping bag, listening to the bugs outside and the growing wind ruffling the trees. They were here to do a job, she reminded herself once again. She also had to keep reminding herself that she wasn't about to start leaning on any other man to help fill a void in her life. Even if that man *was* Ryan Tobias.

She wished she knew what time it was. Sleep had been eluding her for hours, and Ryan still hadn't come back. It crossed her mind that maybe he'd realised the error of his ways and retreated to his own tent after solving whatever emergency problem had come up, but her ego told her otherwise. He wanted her, no matter what. Right? *He'd* been the one who'd initiated everything. He'd approached her in the lake…held her hand by the fire. He'd kissed her.

She put a hand to her lips, swollen and plump from those kisses. Her chin was still tingling in the wake of his stubble.

She pulled the sleeping bag over her head. So much for her being a professional. She needed him next to her *now*. She needed to feel his skin on hers. She wanted him to make love to her so badly she didn't think she'd be able to function otherwise. But where the hell *was* he?

When dawn arrived and she still hadn't slept a wink, she grabbed her toothbrush and water, pulled the zipper up on her tent and crawled outside, yawning. The camp was eerily quiet. Usually there were one or two people milling about, cleaning their teeth outside their tents, doing star jumps to wake themselves up.

She wandered towards the medical stations. The sky wasn't as yellow as it usually was at this time of day. It was a deep, ominous grey, looming large against the tree-tops like the roof of another dark tent. Rain was on the way again, she thought as she spotted a howler monkey leap from one branch overhead to another.

She saw Maria, walking from one station to another. Madeline followed her, pushing back the plastic sheet over the door. 'Morning,' she said.

Maria spun around in surprise, her hands full of the gauzes she was relocating from a box to a table. 'Oh, Madeline, hi—you're up early.'

'I couldn't sleep. Where is…?' She paused, realising she probably shouldn't ask specifically about Ryan. 'Where is everyone?'

'It was kind of a crazy night,' Maria said, and for the first time Madeline noticed the dark circles under her eyes. 'Guy got attacked by a black caiman up the river; the crew left about an hour ago to see to him.'

'Attacked?' Madeline realised she was still holding her toothbrush. She slid it into the pocket of her denim shorts.

'Five metres long, it was—apparently. Guy got too close to her eggs, we're guessing.'

'Is he OK?'

'If you count being alive as "OK" he's OK. They flew him to the hospital and now they're back at the village. The crew wanted to do some filming there, I think. They'll probably be gone awhile.'

Madeline couldn't help the disappointment settling in her stomach like a lead balloon. She felt for whoever had been chomped on by a caiman, of course, but she also felt selfishly resentful of being kept from Ryan even longer.

'Oh, the producer wants to talk to you,' Maria said, making Madeline's heart falter for a second.

'Really? What about?'

She started to pray internally. Had Mark said something about how close she and Ryan had been standing outside her tent when he'd sprung up on them? Were they all writing stories of their own already? Was the producer going to tell her to back off—to be professional or not be there at all?

'I think she wants an interview about the girl you helped yesterday, if that's OK?'

Madeline tried not to sigh out loud in relief. She was way too paranoid. 'I'm sure that will be fine,' she said.

She left Maria sorting her gauzes and made her way back towards her tent. But the heat was already making the air intolerably stuffy and she knew that in a canvas bubble she'd simply sweat and feel uncomfortable.

At the last minute Madeline turned, passed the ashes from the fire and followed the path towards the river. She sometimes liked to wander down and chat in Spanish to the local guys who hung out there, waiting to row people up and down from village to village. Besides, she needed to wake up before the kids started gathering around her for the day. She was so tired. Now that she thought about it, she was actually still in a dream.

'Madeline Savoia, you are officially killing me.'

The longing in his voice as he'd said those words had made a pinball machine of her body, sending hot white sparks zig-zagging downwards from her ears, to her nipples, to her toes.

She'd never been kissed like that before. It had been like something from a movie, she mused, the way he'd reached for her and yanked her forward, pressed his mouth to hers as if she was some kind of lifeline. Maybe she was.

So romantic.

She was halfway to the river when a voice in the trees, slightly in the distance, caught her attention. Stopping in her tracks and yawning sleepily again, she listened closer and heard it yet again. It was a man's voice and it sounded vaguely familiar. One of the crew?

They were probably filming just outside the village. Or maybe there was another emergency. She frowned to herself, feeling stupid. She should be helping them. After what had happened yesterday Madeline was starting to feel she should probably be doing a lot more around camp than simply writing and teaching the kids about cleaning their teeth—much as she loved them.

Maybe she should be assisting in every medical procedure she could, to build her confidence up. Maybe she should even go back to nursing when she returned to London...

Another voice, closer now, yanked her out of her thoughts. She turned towards it, started walking the other pathway towards the noise. As she did so a crash of thunder overhead made her jump. She noticed with dismay that the sky was even darker. She could hear the voices, still ahead of her, and she sped up, clutching her water bottle.

Raindrops started thudding onto the leaves and foliage above her, a few of them slipping through onto her skin. Rain always sounded so much louder in the jungle.

The path was thinning a little. Some way ahead she heard what sounded like the whole team having a heated conversation about something. The rain was too loud for her to make any of the words out, but Madeline was sure there must have been another emergency. She hoped she'd be able to help.

She pushed through a wall of vines and came to a small clearing with what looked like several paths of flattened grass leading away from it in different directions. At the sound of a male voice she carried onwards, and when she turned a small corner she saw them, gathered in a circle, looking down at something on the leaf-strewn ground.

Madeline was just about to call out when she froze in her tracks.

It wasn't the crew.

Her heart leapt straight into her windpipe as she took them in. A group of guys—maybe seven or eight—olive-skinned and covered in black tattoos, some in black shirts, some in white, all studying what she was pretty certain was a dead body. They were speaking quickly amongst themselves, loudly in Spanish, and they hadn't seen her.

Slowly, so as not to make a single branch or twig crack, she stepped backwards, never taking her eyes off them. That was when she saw a flash of metal: an AK-47 being brandished about wildly by a shirtless guy who looked and sounded angry about something.

Drug runners, she thought, trafficking between Colombia and Brazil, no doubt…or planning to. She was almost paralysed with fear. She couldn't be certain that was what they were, but she couldn't hang around to find out.

Somehow she forced herself to move, thankful for the rain now coming down even harder, silencing her footsteps. She found herself back in the clearing, but in a panic realised in horror that she couldn't remember which way she'd come.

She cursed under her breath, hearing movement behind her. The group was getting closer.

Had they heard her?

Which way was the right way?

Feeling nauseous, Madeline started to run. In her hurry she dropped her water bottle, found the path, then ran even faster till her lungs began to burn and the branches slashed at her limbs like an evil army.

As she gasped for air in the suffocating heat she couldn't for the life of her figure out where she was. The path looked the same as the one she'd walked in on, yet it was totally different. She was lost in the jungle.

Fear flooded her veins. The rain pummelled punishingly at her head, arms and legs. Thunder crashed above her and the bugs upped their symphony, as though trying to compete with the noise. She turned and ran back the way she'd come. At least she *thought* it was the way she'd come.

She couldn't hear the voices any more, but then she couldn't hear anything at all—nothing but the rain, and the wind, howling all around her like tortured spirits.

Tears of helplessness brimmed in her eyes. She heard Ryan's voice in her head—the way he'd sounded back when he'd warned her: *'The jungle has a way of luring people in and keeping them.'*

No. *No!* How could she have been so stupid? She had to get out. She had to get back to the camp.

She picked up her pace, but in another second her sandal caught on something long and sharp and she fell hard to the ground, smacking her head. She barely had time to yelp or blink before blackness consumed her.

CHAPTER FIFTEEN

'WHERE'S MADELINE?'

Ryan couldn't keep the question in any longer. He'd been back for over an hour and hadn't seen her playing with the kids under the tree or anywhere else, like she usually was. The guitar was still in the dining room where they'd left it, seemingly untouched, which he found odd because she'd seemed pretty excited about playing it and starting to make up songs.

He'd gone for a swim in the lake the moment the rain had eased off, hoping she might be there, but she wasn't.

'I haven't seen her since this morning,' Maria told him, taking the thermometer from the mouth of the kid who was sitting on the table in front of her.

'This morning?'

'First thing. She was up at dawn, before the storm rolled in. Is she not in her tent?'

Ryan's jaw started to pulse. He didn't want to seem overly concerned but something didn't feel right. He left the station and walked across the wet, muddy grass, sparkling with the remnants of the storm. It was gone four p.m. and it would be dark in a few short hours.

Reaching Madeline's tent, he rapped on the canvas door. No reply.

Without hesitation he unzipped it and looked inside.

Her sleeping bag was in a crumpled heap on the mattress. A can of DEET was resting beside it. He straightened up again, swiftly scanning the swaying treeline.

He saw Mark appearing from his own tent, and walked over. 'Have you seen Madeline?'

'No, sir, not since last night.'

'Call everyone into the dining room, now.' Ryan was already walking towards it quickly.

It didn't take long for word to spread and for everyone on camp to gather in the enclosed space. All wore looks of concern, which unnerved him further. Jake, who'd been following him all day as they'd fixed up the man who'd been mauled by a caiman, was still rolling the camera, obviously sensing excitement in the air.

Ryan took off his baseball hat, dashed his hand through his hair as he tried to force his voice to stay controlled. 'Has anyone here seen Madeline Savoia since this morning?' he asked.

Silence.

He could see people looking around them in confusion. The way Mark was looking at Evan almost made him snap. Others were shaking their heads, looking at the floor.

He turned to Maria. 'Maria, did she say anything about where she was going when she left you?'

Maria shrugged, looked helpless. 'Not a lot…but I was busy. I told her the producer wanted to talk to her and—'

'What did she say when you said that?' he asked, hoping to God Madeline hadn't freaked out and let any paranoia over their…*situation*…get the better of her.

'Nothing, really, just that she was fine with it. She sounded perfectly normal—a little tired, maybe…'

'Tired?'

'She said she didn't sleep much.'

Ryan rarely panicked, but he was panicking now. Madeline was exhausted and had obviously wandered off somewhere. That could only lead to bad things in the jungle. Maybe she'd been caught in the storm. Anything could have happened.

'We're splitting up and we're going to find her,' he said resolutely. 'Evan, Mark—go back to the village. Take the sat phones. Maria, go with Pablo to the river, get on the boat and keep your eyes peeled. Take your sat phone, too—everyone take your sat phones…keep in touch…'

Ryan doled out responsibilities, then watched his people hurrying off two by two until he was the only one left—just him and Jake with the camera.

He grabbed some bananas, raced to his tent and lifted his pack, slinging it over his shoulders. 'I'll be right out,' he called to Jake. 'Actually, can you grab some more water and meet me back here?'

'No problem.'

Jake turned back the way they'd come and Ryan took his moment to flee alone.

Anger, fear and dread propelled him forward as he set out on the path, fixing his phone to the belt of his khaki trousers. He'd been in this situation before, and he did *not* need a camera filming his every movement. He did *not* need anyone seeing anything they didn't need to see, if that was what this was going to come to.

He hoped to hell it wasn't.

Josephine's face flashed to the forefront of his mind, bright and smiling, then pale and cold. He bit down hard on the inside of his cheek, fought to keep his breathing steady and his feet treading safely, quickly on the path.

This day wouldn't end up like that one had—not if he had anything to do with it. It *couldn't*. He couldn't handle it again. He'd barely handled it before. And even now, with the faint glimmer of sunshine that was Madeline on the horizon, those demons were still dancing around him in the darkness, willing him to slip up or break.

He called her name. The air was thick, hot, suffocating.

Keeping tabs on his own whereabouts, he crossed the clearing. His phone buzzed and squawked. He could hear people talking over the radio. His crew were all out there, spread like a spider's web between the trees. The village had their people out now, too, but no one had seen her yet.

He was just about to take another step when he paused in front of an object. He bent down, picked up a toothbrush. It was one of the same branded batch they'd brought with them for the kids. One that Madeline would have had. He shoved it into a pocket.

A shape up ahead caught his eye next. He stopped in his tracks, waiting for it to move.

'Madeline?'

He stepped closer cautiously, adrenaline pumping through him. It was a person—a woman, he realised with sudden nausea—lying still on the ground like a fallen log, rain-soaked and lifeless in an unnatural heap.

Ryan's heart plunged as he hurried to her side. She was facing away from him, and he saw with utter horror the pool of blood spreading like a crimson lake from her stomach out onto the muddy, mossy ground.

He fell to his knees as his very soul seemed to splinter around him.

'Madeline?' A whisper now. His voice barely audible.

Long dark hair was splayed across the woman's face, hiding her features, and he felt like throwing up. He put a hand to her cheek. Cold, clammy. She was gone. He swallowed the sob that rose in his throat. He hadn't deserved her. He knew it. He never had.

He pushed the hair back from her face, ready to haul her into his arms and let grief consume him, but shock froze him as her features came into view. The rounded nose, the plump lips, the thick, bushy eyebrows.

It wasn't Madeline.

This poor woman had been murdered. There was no doubt about that. But she wasn't Madeline.

Ryan stood up quickly and almost stumbled as he reached for his penknife and readied himself to wield it against an attacker. He swiped at his tears, spun around, half expecting a Colombian drug runner to lunge in his direction. But all he could hear was the wind and the birds and the distant howl of a monkey.

With his eyes on the treeline he pulled his sat phone from his belt, radioed in his grim discovery, reading out the GPS location so the crew could come back for her and carried on, on his way, hope his motivation.

The light was fading and the wind was picking up again—like the rain. He knew another shower was on its way and prayed it wouldn't be as bad as the last one. He'd changed course now and was only a few metres back from the river. This was far enough away so that Madeline would never be spotted by Maria and Pablo from the boat, but not so far... Madeline might have gone just a little off track and thought she was further away from camp than she really was.

He let out a silent prayer. The rain started pattering more heavily on his hat and Ryan struggled to keep it together.

'Any luck?' It was Mark on the radio.

'Not yet,' he replied, trying to sound optimistic. 'She can't have gone far.'

But he heard his own voice crack in despair.

It was happening all over again.

He was just about to sink to the ground when he saw her. He almost dropped his phone. She was huddled under a tree, arms wrapped around herself, her eyes closed.

'Madeline!'

He was in front of her in a heartbeat, kneeling on the ground, letting the rain slam into him as he pulled his pack from his back, dropping it next to her.

'Madeline, it's me—look at me.'

He reached his hands to her face, hoping her cheeks wouldn't be as cold as those of the lifeless lady he'd just touched. To his utter relief her eyes fluttered open just a little. There was blood on her head, trickling down her right cheek and onto his hands. She looked dazed.

'What happened?' he asked, scooting even closer to her, inspecting the damage. 'Can you talk? Are you in pain?'

'Ryan?' Recognition flickered in her eyes before they flooded with tears. She reached out to him and wrapped her arms around his shoulders.

She could move, thank God. Her arms were weak but that hug, along with the sound of her voice, was everything he needed in that moment. He held her tight against him for a minute, swallowed more tears in private against her soft neck, then untangled her from him.

'I don't know what the *hell* you were thinking,' he blurted, sweeping her matted hair behind her ears, scanning her eyes, hearing his own voice croak again. 'Didn't I tell you *never* to go anywhere alone out here? Maddy, you could've been *killed*! Didn't I tell you...? Weren't you listening?'

'I'm sorry... I'm so sorry...'

'I could have lost you, too.'

He held her face, pressed his lips to her forehead for

a long moment, letting them burn into her skin, breathing in her life at the same time.

'I didn't know what I was going to find.'

'Drug runners,' she whispered, clutching his hand and wincing as she tried to move again. 'I saw them. I think they killed someone, Ryan.'

'I think you're right about that. Now we need to get you cleaned up.'

It looked as though she'd fallen and hit her head at some point. She was covered in mud, too, and had probably dragged herself to the tree after her fall. She was clearly disorientated, and likely dehydrated.

He reached for his pack, pulled out a bottle of water and held it to her mouth. 'You need to drink, Maddy,' he said. 'As much as you can.'

With her eyes closed she did as she was told. Remembering the sat phone, he announced that he'd found her, and told the crew his co-ordinates. As he was talking he noticed that the insect bites on her legs and arms had caused her limbs to swell. She'd obviously come out without DEET on again. Either that or it had been washed off.

He was amazed she wasn't more hurt.

The rain was coming down hard again and Ryan knew it was going to be hell, trying to make it back to camp with her like this. He reached into his pack and pulled out the thin plastic sheet, stood and shook it out. It took him less than two minutes to hang it between three surrounding branches, creating a makeshift shelter. He pulled another sheet out and laid it on the ground, helped her onto it and sat close beside her.

At least they were dry, for now.

'What's that?' she asked, watching him pull tincture from his pack, along with some swabs and gauze.

'Iodine,' he said, holding it up. 'Here, let me look at you. You're still bleeding.'

He placed two fingers under her chin and she balled his shirt in her fists against his chest as he swabbed at the cut on her head, then applied antiseptic.

She screwed up her face. 'Stings,' she said.

'I'm not surprised. Did you pass out?'

'For a bit, I think. I was trying to get away from them. I heard them behind me, then I got lost. I feel like such an idiot. I'm so sorry, Ryan.'

'Not as sorry as *I'd* have been if anything worse had happened to you. You must have lost them, but there's a dead woman not far from here. I think they left her there.'

He started to apply a patch to the wound, but Madeline pulled back, putting a hand over her mouth.

'So they *did* kill someone?'

He nodded grimly. 'I saw her. We're retrieving the body.'

Her eyes were wide. 'I saw them standing around her. I saw a gun.'

'She was stabbed,' he said, grateful again for the miraculous fact that the same fate hadn't befallen her. He pulled a banana out of his pack. 'Eat this—you must be starving.'

He swabbed at some of the blood on her arms and legs with a cloth. Thankfully most of it had come from her head and the rest of her was unharmed except for the bites.

'We'll wait the rain out, then we'll get you back. Why did you walk off on your own?'

'I thought I might be able to help with a case. I thought I heard you talking, but it wasn't you. I can't believe… That poor woman. Why would they do that?'

'Any number of reasons. They make up their own rules out here.'

He pulled her to his side, wrapped an arm around her shoulders protectively as she ate and drank slowly, both of them listening to the rain. As the crickets chirped and the bats started swooping he felt the frantic thudding of his heart finally begin to subside.

'What happened with the guy who got attacked by the caiman?' Madeline asked.

Ryan stretched his legs out on the sheet. 'He wasn't as lucky as you—lost most of one arm. Luckily he had a friend with him who was able to call for help when it happened.'

She grimaced.

'We're just skin and blood and bones in the jungle, I guess,' he said, resting a cheek against her hair. 'We're all the same. We're all just food in a chain. Moving targets.'

'Terrifying, isn't it?' she said softly.

'Terrifying.'

He tightened his arm around her small frame, banishing the thought from his mind that Madeline might have been the one mauled or eaten or shot.

Ryan hadn't even known it was within him to feel so responsible, to feel so...*anything* about anyone, until today. The depth of his feelings now—the way they'd sprung upon him around this woman—was as terrifying as the jungle. But it also made him feel incredibly alive. More alive, perhaps, than he'd felt in five whole years.

CHAPTER SIXTEEN

MADELINE WATCHED THEM bringing the body of the murdered woman into the camp from her place on the bench in the dining room. Through the mesh of the walls she could make out Ryan, Jake and the producer, plus two volunteers carrying the stretcher across the grass.

They'd been informed it was a lady from another village, probably employed to traffic drugs up the river. She tore her eyes away as tears blurred her vision, pulling the blanket around her for comfort. Shock was sinking in now that she was finally safe.

She also felt impossibly idiotic.

She'd never been more relieved to see anyone in her whole life than she had when Ryan had found her under that tree. He'd been angry at first—that much she understood. She could hardly blame him. She'd gone against everything he'd told her when she'd stepped off that path and followed what she'd thought were her instincts.

She knew half of his anger was coming from a place of fear, though: fear of her being hurt. He'd shown her nothing but kindness ever since.

The ibuprofen Ryan had given her had taken some of her aches away, and a soothing gel had stopped her bites from itching. She'd eaten what she could of a plate of white rice and vegetables, but thoughts of what might have happened to her out there kept careening through her mind like a crazy carousel, making her feel sick.

She put her fork down, pushed through the thin mesh door and walked outside to the fire, now blazing.

Maria held an arm out to her, beckoning her to sit next to her on the log. 'Did you eat?' she asked.

'I did, thank you.'

'How are you feeling now?'

'Stupid,' she answered honestly, staring at the flames.

Maria rested her head on her shoulder for a second, then smiled. 'Honey, we all make mistakes. We're just glad you're all right. It's a good thing Ryan sent the search party out when he did. It's just so crazy busy here that things can sometimes get overlooked...'

'It was *his* call to get everyone out looking for me?' she asked. She'd had no clue.

'He was the first to realise no one had seen you in a while.'

When Madeline turned towards Maria she noticed something in the older woman's tired eyes that she hadn't seen before. A slight twinkle.

'You're good for him,' Maria whispered, conspiratorially. 'Whatever it is you're doing, keep doing it.'

Madeline flushed, shook her head, but she didn't have time to respond before she felt a firm hand on her shoulder from behind. The next second Ryan was stepping over the log, crouching down in front of her, his handsome face in shadow, blocking the fire.

'Hey, how's your head now?'

He reached for the bandage over her wound to check it, and instinctively she brought her own up to cover his hand.

'I'll live,' she said, moving his hand down to her lap as he smiled in what looked like relief. Gratitude overwhelmed her. 'I can't thank you enough for coming to find me, Ryan—for sending everyone out to find me. Don't think I'll ever forget that.'

She reached out a hand to Maria, too, and as she looked between them she was flooded with warmth and the purest of appreciation for everything she had. Everything that the poor woman who'd lost her life out there would never have.

'I'm going to go back to nursing when I get home,' she announced. 'I want to finish what I started. For Toby.'

Maria squeezed her hand. Ryan raised his eyebrows as he sat on his haunches and tossed a stick into the fire. 'Good to hear it,' he said.

'You have no idea how inspiring you all are.'

'Well, thank you, honey,' Maria said, sounding pleased and a little embarrassed. 'Who's Toby?'

Madeline ran a hand through her tangled hair. It was weird, but she didn't feel as uncomfortable talking about him any more.

'Toby is the reason I'm here.'

As the words left her mouth she realised it was true. That little boy's death had forced her to run away from her duties...possibly even from her destiny.

She loved writing—she'd stumbled into it and had been blessed to have had adventures all around the world because of it—but it was still a means of escape. And in escaping she'd wound up here.

How strange.

She tilted her head up to the sky, to the stars. Had Toby planned this out? Anything was possible, she supposed. The longer she spent in the jungle, away from technology and crowds and confusing messages coming at her from every which way, the more she felt connected to the universe. The more she resonated with the truths she *couldn't* see.

The only things that were real, she decided, were the things she could hold in her heart.

Ryan was looking at her when she opened her eyes. He got to his feet, helping her to stand. 'You should rest,' he told her, his grey eyes full of concern.

'Goodnight—sleep tight,' Maria said, after giving her a hug, and Madeline didn't miss the surreptitious little wink she threw her in the firelight as Ryan led her away.

'I need a bath,' she said, halfway across the grass, pulling on his hand in the direction of the lake.

He looked back to camp—for the cameras, she assumed. Luckily there were none in sight.

'Come with me? I can't sleep like this.'

'I probably shouldn't,' he said, looking around them again warily.

But she was already guiding him down the path, through the trees and onto the deck. The moon was clear now the rain had gone, sending bright white beams across the black expanse of water so there was no need for a flashlight. The trees rustled overhead and the bats were swooping, catching flies. So peaceful.

She peeled off her shorts, then her muddied tank top, dropping them at her feet. Ryan was standing in front of her, watching her in what looked like wonder while taking off his boots. She smiled at him with newfound confidence, then stepped closer, reached for his shirt and motioned for him to lift his arms. With ease she pulled it over his head, shuddering as his hands landed on her waist and his lips grazed the top of her head.

'You're amazing—do you know that?' he whispered into her hair.

'So are you.'

'Infuriating…'

She grinned. 'So are you.'

'I kind of think I need you, though.'

His bare skin so close to hers sent shockwaves pulsing through Madeline's body. She pressed her hands to his chest, tilted her head up for his kiss, let her fingers trail down towards his khaki trousers and undid them quickly. He slid them off his legs, followed by his boxers. Then, when he'd swiftly undone her bra and tossed it to the side, he got to his knees, naked in front of her, dropped butterfly kisses around her belly button and slid her underwear down past her knees, over her feet and to the floor.

She gasped as he kissed his way back up, lingering on her inner thigh, running his hands up her legs as he did so.

'Let's get in,' he said, reaching for her hand.

They slid off the deck and into the water. Madeline was careful not to dunk her head, and to keep her bandage dry.

The water was a cool, blissful blanket, wrapping around her hot skin as Ryan reached for the bar of soap someone had left on the lakeside. He guided her out a little further, then pulled her back to his chest, kissing her neck from behind as he ran the soap over her chest. She held her arms out and he did the same to them.

The insect bites all over her skin were extra-sensitive, but strangely she found his gentle touch turned the irritation into something almost sensual. Madeline turned in his arms, returning his passionate kisses, and wrapped her legs around his middle. He held her up with ease, kissing her hungrily, and for a moment she wondered what they must look like from afar, chest to chest in the middle of a lake under the moon.

Take the drug runners and the dead body and the fact

that she herself might have died today out of the equation and she couldn't help thinking that this was the greatest day of her whole life.

She grinned against his lips in spite of herself.

'What are you thinking?' he asked curiously, trailing the soap up and down her back.

'How life is pure magic,' she said.

He smiled into her eyes. 'That, right there, Madeline, is why I...like you.'

Madeline pressed her lips to his again, drawing him into another deep kiss, running her hands through his wet hair. He'd left a gap before saying 'like'. Had he been going to say something else?

Her heart thudded against his. It was trying its hardest to jump out of her skin. Of course he hadn't, she scolded herself.

She thought about the way she felt about him, the giddy smile he left on her face. She thought about the way he'd held her and helped her today, the way he'd all but forced her to face her fears about performing any kind of medical duty. Ryan had changed her life already...maybe even *saved* her life. And now they were kissing madly like teenagers in a lake, and there was nowhere else on earth she'd rather be...

They gathered up their clothes, and Ryan gave her his shirt to wear. Clutching the rest, they sneaked back the way they'd come, making absolutely certain not to be seen. There wasn't any discussion about where they'd be sleeping. Ryan simply looked around one more time outside his tent, unzipped the canvas door and motioned for her to crawl inside.

He crawled in after her, zipped up the door again behind them, and in a second it was just the two of them in the tiny enclosed space. Madeline's heart was doing back-flips.

He flattened out the sheets on his mattress accommodatingly, so she could lie down, then leaned over her on one arm and inspected her head. Just his palm against her cheek, then against the back of her head, had her breathing more heavily again in a second.

'We should change the dressing on that,' he said, reaching behind him for his bag.

She sat up and he pulled her legs around him so she was straddling him, and in the light of his flashlight he carefully reapplied the bandage over her cut with the skill she'd seen a hundred times on all those online videos.

Starstruck, she thought, *and at the mercy of his nimble fingers*. She *was* starstruck, but it was more than that now. He was a different person from the man she'd literally fallen into back in London. To her he was anyway.

When he was done he turned the light off, plunging them into darkness once again. Madeline reached her hands to his stubbled jaw, stroked his face and dropped kisses onto the edges of his mouth.

'Thank you,' she whispered.

Her legs wrapped more tightly around him of their own accord. In less than twenty seconds he somehow removed his shirt from her damp body, and everything from himself. Carefully he lowered her onto her back on the sheets, traced his fingers around her collarbone and down her stomach with a touch so light it left her skin a mass of tingles.

'How are you feeling now?' he asked, replacing his fingers with his lips and trailing kisses along her skin, back up to her mouth.

Madeline wrapped her arms around him from beneath,

pulling him closer. 'Better, Doctor,' she breathed. 'A little bit better every second, actually.'

He continued his kissing trail, teasing her, driving her crazy. By the time he reached her inner thighs she was practically about to explode, but he stopped every now and then, found her lips again, and then let her flip him onto his back and sit astride him.

Madeline knew she had him in the palm of her hands...literally.

He groaned.

'Shh,' she teased, pulling away and flattening her hands against his chest, tracing his muscles, relishing every sinewy stretch of his amazing body. She was conscious suddenly that the wall separating their antics from the outside world was a millimetre thick and not exactly soundproof.

'It's pretty hard to be quiet when you're doing that,' he growled, and she pressed her lips to his again, silencing him.

The tent was hot, and already their bodies were melding together as one with perspiration. The bugs were still singing in the night outside. The wind whipped about the canvas every now and then like a jealous lover trying to get in. Her head was starting to hurt again, where she'd fallen, but when Ryan reached for his bag again and unwrapped a condom Madeline was beyond caring about *anything*.

'You carry these?' she asked in surprise, taking it from him and rolling it on.

He put his hands to her waist, lifted her with ease and flipped her onto her back again.

'Not for me,' he said in a low voice, resting on his hands either side of her and sucking on her lower lip for a second.

She moaned quietly as desire rocketed through her.

'Sometimes the crew need them. Sometimes we give them to the teenagers.'

'How generous,' she said, kissing him deeply as her legs encircled him from beneath once more.

She lost herself in their kiss again, in their twirling tongues and clashing teeth and soft moans and groans, until she gasped, biting on her own hand.

'Does it hurt?' he said softly, pausing, stroking her hair against the thin pillow.

'No, don't be silly. I just don't want to scream.'

'They'll just think you've seen a spider.'

'Very funny.'

'Seriously, Madeline, you feel incredible.'

Tears sprang to her eyes from out of nowhere and she wished it wasn't quite so dark. She was beyond exhausted and yet she was making love to Ryan Tobias—slowly, gently, beautifully in their own little bubble. There was so much admiration in his words and in his tone she felt it settle into her skin, deep into her bones.

He took his time, being careful not to hurt her any further after her ordeal, she was sure, but the result of his concern was something so passionate, so sensual she had literally never made love quite like it. Whatever he wasn't saying he was showing as he stroked and caressed her, kissed her everywhere he could reach over and over and over.

She reciprocated, of course, limited only by the space in the tent, and when Madeline woke up the next morning with his arms wrapped tightly around her she couldn't even remember when they'd finally stopped—or how, or why, or in which position. All she knew was that she'd never felt so worshipped in her whole life.

She also knew she was probably in deep trouble.

CHAPTER SEVENTEEN

RYAN WAS STANDING outside the medical station watching Madeline strumming the guitar under a tree. Her made-up songs were proving a hit. He couldn't be sure but he thought that right now she was singing something about cars on motorways, in Spanish. At any rate, the kids were squealing and singing along as if they'd never heard anything so fantastic.

He smiled, quashing the urge to walk over and join in. Of course hiding their relationship...or whatever it was that had blossomed between them since their first amazing night together in his tent...had not been easy.

Luckily they spent enough time together professionally to warrant her hanging out with him in the lake, and in his hammock, and in the boat on the river without too much need for explanation.

The boat had become a favourite of theirs. They liked to take a couple of blankets out with them, fish for piranhas and talk under the stars. Then they'd spend long hours making love to the sounds of the jungle, with the sighs of each other's pleasure mingling with the wind.

He pushed his hand into his pocket, remembering that first morning he'd woken up with his chest glued to her back with sweat. Instead of feeling panicked, he'd felt remarkably calm. Maddy had entered his life like a hurricane, but somehow settled like a soft blanket of snow, silencing everything, instilling peace amongst the chaos of his busy mind.

The short weeks since they'd been strangers were blurred in his head now; all he knew was the curve of her smile, the feel of her soft tongue dancing circles with his, the sound of her laugher.

'She adores them,' Maria said, appearing next to him from the tent and nudging his shoulder. 'She's going to find it hard to leave them, I'll bet.'

He straightened, sipped from his water bottle, suddenly aware that he'd been staring at Madeline—probably with a sappy look on his face.

'I'm sure she will,' he said, clearing his throat and screwing the bottle cap back on. 'She'll miss them a lot.'

'They're not the only ones, it seems,' she added, nudging him again, and then slipping back into the medical station with a new patient before he could respond.

He frowned to himself.

No one had asked any questions—although admittedly he hadn't missed the looks and the little comments thrown his way by Maria, Mark and Evan.

Aside from their affair, though, Ryan was rather enjoying watching a transformation occur in Madeline. She was more determined than ever to return to her position at St David's Hospital once she got home, so was spending even more time with the kids, helping them read in English and assisting in as many medical duties concerning them as possible. She was soaking it all up like a sponge.

And at night they soaked each other up, wherever and whenever they could, for as long as humanly possible, until they fell asleep exhausted.

Last night had been no exception. She'd found him in the hammock after dinner in the twilight.

'Are you really reading my book?' she'd asked, taking the e-reader from his hands.

Her hair had been damp from a previous swim—a swim he'd had to let her take alone, thanks to a visit from the wife of the man who'd been attacked by a caiman—she'd bought him a thank-you box of fruit. More bananas...

'Of course I'm reading it. I like it,' he'd told her truthfully. 'You have quite a way with words.'

'Well, I should hope so. I'm a writer,' she'd said, taking the Kindle from him and climbing into the hammock alongside him.

It had stretched almost to the floor with their weight, and she had smiled contentedly with her head against his chest.

'Lucky this is the king of all hammocks,' she'd said.

He'd laughed, peeling the strap of her tank top away from her shoulder and kissing her soft, warm flesh. When darkness had fallen they'd made love right there in the hammock—a feat he hadn't even known was entirely possible.

Ryan had never been so turned on in his life than he had been by the sight of Madeline, sliding her underwear off beneath her sundress, raising her arms above him to clutch at the mesh, and she'd relished every moan he'd let slip from his mouth as she worked him up and then slowed her pace again, then sped up, driving him crazy.

He'd almost forgotten to keep an eye on the treeline for the crew, and for Jake with his damn camera, but they'd grown good at multi-tasking by now—and besides, he was in too deep to care.

He watched her now, putting the guitar down on the

grass between the kids, strolling over towards him. His heart leapt and he rolled his eyes at himself.

Way too deep, he repeated internally. There was no way out either.

He was considering asking her to accompany him on another shoot...in a medical capacity, of course. They were headed for Peru in a couple of weeks, and after that to Bali. Maybe she could extend her deadline for the memoir.

The memoir she still hadn't finished because of him.

He silenced the thought.

'Hey,' she said, stopping in front of him.

Her hair was pulled back into a ponytail and he saw the faint red outline of the mark on her head from where she'd fallen. It had healed nicely in his care.

'Hey,' he said back, meeting her eyes and feeling that familiar rush of adrenaline shoot through his veins. He was still getting used to the feelings she stirred in him—a reawakening of sorts.

'We're wrapping up for the morning. Now I need another interview with you,' she said, biting on her lip.

He raised his eyebrows, appraising her in her green dress, seeing the way it was already sticking to her sexily in the heat.

'Do you think you'll have time for a quick one?'

He knew what *that* meant, and as usual he was a moth to her flame. 'Can we do it in the waterfall?' he asked, stifling a smile.

She was struggling to keep the laughter off her face, but it was shining in her eyes. 'I'd *love* to do it in the waterfall.'

'Great.' He called out to Maria. 'I'm taking a break!'

Luckily he'd put his board shorts on under his scrubs...

They walked a metre apart from one another across camp, until they reached another clearing. One of the local guys had introduced them all to the secret waterfall just a ten-minute walk along a hidden path the last time they'd been here, and as soon as they were out of sight of anyone from camp he wrapped his arms around Madeline, picked her up and ran the rest of the way, jumping over the branches and piles of fallen leaves on the way.

She laughed as her arms latched around his neck. 'You just *love* to feel like Tarzan out here, don't you?'

'What makes you say that?' he said, putting her down on the grassy slope that led down to the pool and beating his chest as he faced the water.

He watched her peeling off the green dress, revealing her purple bikini as she waded into the cool, murky pool. She was being careful not to step on the sharp rocks, just as they'd been shown. The pool was only ten or so metres wide, but the water rolling dramatically off the high rocks above it was pretty much the perfect disguise for the sounds of mutual enjoyment.

He knew that *she* knew that was what he hoped was about to happen now. She was teasing him, though.

'I meant it when I said I needed another interview,' she said, turning back to him and observing him ditching his shorts.

Her eyes never left his naked body in the sunlight as he followed her into the water.

'I know you've been avoiding the subject—putting me to work on other things, thinking I'll forget what I really came here to do. It's what you've been doing all along.'

She pulled her long hair from its ponytail and ran her hands through it. Then she dipped into the water and floated on her back. *Damn*, she was sexy as hell.

'That's not entirely true,' he said, meeting her in the middle and running a hand up her leg, letting his fingers brush the soft fabric of her bikini bottoms.

He'd tease her for a few minutes at least, he thought, before lifting her up onto one of the flat, long rocks behind the falls and using the rest of their 'break' in a very constructive fashion.

She didn't move—didn't respond to his touch in the way he'd been hoping she would. Instead she spun round and wrapped her legs around his stomach, pulling him in. He was trapped, completely in her control, and he liked it.

'You know, it won't be long before we leave this place,' she said, moving her arms around his neck.

'You want to talk about that? What happens next... away from the Amazon?' he asked, ignoring the caution in her voice and what he knew was inevitably coming.

He moved his hands to her bottom and pulled her even closer, dropped a lingering kiss on her lips.

'I've been thinking about it, Maddy. You and me. The future.'

'You have?'

'Of course I have. In case you hadn't noticed, I think you're kind of OK.'

She smiled playfully. 'I think *you're* kind of OK, too—in a weird, moody way. But that's not what we need to talk about right now and you know it.'

He sighed, trying not to show his frustration. Something was ready for action, and he wanted to make love to her right here and now, but he could see he'd have to earn that privilege.

'Talk to me, Ryan. Talk to me about Josephine.'

His chest tightened at the sound of her name. He swam with Madeline's legs and arms still around him over to the waterfall, dipped them both under the surface and brought them up again behind the falls.

'I told you—I don't want to talk about that.'

She let him go, put her feet to the ground and swept her mass of wet hair back over her shoulders. The water was rolling off her eyelashes, down her nose.

'Ryan, not telling me what happened with her feels the same as you lying to me, somehow.'

He pressed his back to the rocks. 'It's *not* the same, I haven't lied to you, Maddy—not once.'

'It *feels* like you have. Why can't you talk about Josephine? *Why?* This has been going on long enough.'

'Don't say her name—and don't write her name in this memoir, please,' he said, closing his eyes again and raking his hands through his wet hair.

'Forget the memoir.'

'What do you mean, forget the memoir?'

'Ryan, it's *me* you're talking to.'

He curled his fists to his sides, dunked down in the water to his neck as Madeline floated in front of him with the cascade of the waterfall behind her.

So many damn questions. Why the hell couldn't she just be a nurse…a normal goddamn nurse with no ulterior motives…a nurse he could hold flat against these rocks and lose himself in completely?

He opened his eyes as he felt her straddling him again, sitting across his lap under the water.

'Forget the book,' she said again, against his lips. 'I'm going back to nursing anyway.' She bunched tufts of his wet hair in her hands.

'I see. So I tell you all my secrets off the record, and then what? You write them down anyway?'

Madeline was silent.

'They're pretty juicy. We'd definitely get a bestseller you wouldn't be able to resist.'

He put his hands to her waist, but she shoved them away.

'Do you *really* think I would do that to you?' Her voice was furious now.

She started clambering off his lap but he pulled her back to him.

'Plenty would. Think of the money.'

'Seriously? Is *that* the kind of person you think I am? You think I'd get involved with you to get some *secret* out of you for my own benefit? Let me go!'

She went to clamber off him again, but he reached a hand to the back of her neck and pulled her head against his, pinning her in place.

'You're sexy when you're mad.'

'That's insulting. Get your hands *off* me!'

'You *like* my hands on you—remember?'

He pressed his lips to hers and she groaned, kissing him back for a moment, letting her arms move around his shoulder blades. But all too soon she pushed him away again, putting a hand to her mouth as if to block him from trying anything else.

She shook her head, her face still only an inch from his. 'No. I can't do this. Do you think because you're some kind of celebrity I'll just take whatever part of you I can get?'

'Of course I don't… Come on, I was kidding.'

'This is *serious*. I want to finish this memoir for *you*— so you can be *free*, Ryan! So you can put this whole thing to rest the way *you* want to by telling the story. I don't have to write it at all—we both know I don't!'

'Then don't.'

'Fine, I won't. But will you still tell me what happened with Josephine?'

'I...' He closed his mouth. He couldn't read her.

'Tell me right now. Tell me because you *trust* me, Ryan. And because you want a future with me. You just said that's what you want. And I'd rather have you than some book that's not even in my name!'

His head was spinning. Josephine's face was right in front of him now, in his mind, laughing, smiling. Then crying. Then cold and lifeless. His fault. *His fault.*

'If you can't trust me we can't be together. There is no future for us. We can't do...*this*!' She gestured around them.

Her face changed—hardened as if she was battling something internally.

'I'm going to ask them to fly me out of here early.'

A laugh spluttered out of him suddenly. 'Right!'

Her expression hardened further.

He stared at her for a second, feeling panic start to rise. 'You can't just leave,' he said, watching her push through the falls. He followed quickly.

'There's no point in me being here one second longer. You've been pushing me and pushing me, Ryan, but you won't give an inch yourself!'

'I've given you plenty of inches,' he said, too quickly, but she wasn't laughing at his jokes any more. 'Maddy, listen. I want to give you everything, I really do. You deserve that. But...'

'But—there's always a *but*. You won't let me in—you won't tell me anything that matters. I feel like you won't share the *real* you! You can't keep leading people on and then pushing them away when closeness gets inconvenient for you, Ryan.'

'I just... It will change the way you think of me.'

'No, it won't.'

'Yes, it will, Maddy…'

'Then don't try and stop me when I go.'

She turned again and he watched helplessly as she gathered up her clothes and hurried up the path. He floated onto his back, breathing deeply, anger pulsing through his body.

If he followed, he'd cause a scene on camp.

Was she testing him?

He counted to ten. Then twenty. Anger turned to apathy. Then confusion. Then back to anger and then fear. He counted to twenty all over again, floated there, festering in his own thoughts, for what felt like hours.

In reality it was probably only half an hour. Then, feeling like a total idiot, he swam so hard back through the water he practically dislocated his shoulders.

The second he pushed through the trees to camp a young volunteer with a name badge reading 'Raul' ran up to him, looking panicked and out of breath.

'There you are! Everyone's been looking for you.'

Crap.

'What's happened?' He was only wearing board shorts—suspiciously dry, he realised, after his 'swim'.

He started walking towards his tent with Raul scurrying at his side.

'Emergency up river. They think it's the drug runners again. We heard gunshots and everyone left…'

'What?' He stopped for a second. This was insane. 'Everyone's gone?'

'Pretty much,' Raul said. 'I was told to wait here for you. We need to set up in case they bring people back. They could only take limited supplies with them.'

Ryan reached his tent, unzipped the door and threw his shirt inside as dread settled around him, making his stomach sink. 'I'll meet you at the station.'

Raul sped off and Ryan bent to crawl inside. He stopped almost instantly. Madeline was emerging from her own tent, complete with her bags. She was fully dressed—boots and all.

Panic seized his heart. 'Madeline?'

She ignored him, started walking quickly across the grass towards the path to the river, swinging her heavy pack over her shoulder as she went.

He ran after her. 'Where are you going?'

'I've arranged for a boat to take me back to Saint Elena.' Her voice was steely, cold as ice.

'Now?' He was incredulous.

'Yes, now.'

'Do you know what has just *happened*?'

'I do, and I'm sorry, but I need to get out of here, Ryan.'

He caught her arm. He was still just in his board shorts, no shoes on his feet, no shirt. He felt powerless. 'Don't go, Maddy. Not now.'

'Don't make this any harder, please, Ryan.' Tears glistened in her eyes but she swiped them away defiantly. 'This is the best time for me to go. No cameras...no one asking questions.'

They were on the pathway now. He could see the river through the trees. The local guys she often talked with were sitting in the boat, laughing about something, waiting for her. What the hell was going on? His world had folded in on itself in a matter of seconds. She couldn't just leave everyone...she couldn't just leave *him*.

'Madeline—'

He shut his mouth the second he'd said her name, let out a yelp, then an anguished cry. He staggered backwards, then pushed her away so hard she fell down, weighted by her pack.

'Don't move,' he managed, and looked back just in time

to see the long, thick-scaled, stripy brown and black snake he'd stepped on slithering away into the undergrowth.

'Did it bite you?' Madeline was scrambling to her feet in the dirt. Her eyes were on the tail end of the snake. 'Oh, my God, did it get you?'

Her voice was shaky. She shook off her pack and was at his side in a second, hands on his shoulders as he sank to the ground.

'Ryan!'

'It got me,' he said, sucking in a breath. 'Surucucu. Madeline, I need the anti-venom.'

He doubled over for a second. The pain was shooting up his leg already. Madeline stood up quickly, calling to the guys near the boat.

'Help! Over here, please!'

'They won't be able to help me…you need to go back to the camp…find Raul.' The guys were already running from the river towards them. '*Go*, Madeline!'

'OK, hold on—OK.' She kissed him quickly on the mouth. 'I'm so sorry…just hold on. I'll be right back!'

She pushed her pack towards him so he could rest on it and sped off back down the path.

On the ground, Ryan grabbed his bare foot and studied the two fang marks just above his ankle. He winced in pain. Sweat had broken out all over his body. The Surucucu's venom took less than two hours to finish someone off. He'd seen it before—the after-effects on soft tissue at least. The venom was a powerful haemotoxin and, thanks to some of the longest fangs on any snake, it had been injected deep into his bloodstream.

He sucked in another breath, tried to focus.

But he knew in his gut that he was running out of time.

CHAPTER EIGHTEEN

'HELP!' MADELINE RAN into the clearing. 'Raul! Anyone?'

She was panicked, desperate, but silence greeted her. Everyone was gone. Raul, too, it seemed. She spun around, calling out again, but clearly no one heard her because no one came.

Ryan's face flashed to the forefront of her mind. He'd turned ashen so quickly. The fang marks on his ankle had been deep and pronounced. It wasn't good and it was all *her* fault. She'd caused him to run after her barefoot, she'd been acting stupidly and melodramatically, and now... Now there was no one to help her or Ryan.

She called out again, shaking like a leaf.

Please, please, please...

Then she remembered something. Ryan had antivenom. He'd shown it to her the first night they'd got here. He'd even shown her how to apply it—not that she'd wanted to know.

She raced to his tent, pulled it open, threw herself inside and grabbed his bag.

Adrenaline propelled her forward, back the way she'd come.

'Hold on, hold on...' she said two minutes later, dropping to his side on the ground and resting her hand on his knee. He looked grey. He was leaning on her pack. 'Stay with me, Ryan! Can you hear me?'

Two guys from the river were sitting either side of him, holding his arms.

'We should not move him,' they told her in Spanish. 'We don't want the venom to spread.'

'OK, hold him steady.'

His eyes were heavy, drooping now. Sweat was glistening on his forehead and the snakebite was swollen, making his leg look twice its size. He clutched her hand for a second. He could barely speak, she could tell. She tried to stay calm, desperately channelling her inner nurse.

'I've got your bag,' she told him, pulling her hand away and opening it up in front of her. The contents spilled to the ground. 'Tell me how to help you, Ryan.'

'Anti-venom,' he mumbled. He was clearly struggling to keep his eyes open.

'I know, but which one?'

Madeline stared at the vials and tubes, the syringes and creams and containers. She recognised the anti-venoms, but there were several, all intended for different bites. She held one up to show him.

'This one?' she said.

He shook his head weakly, trying and failing to focus on the spread on the floor.

'This one?' she said, holding up another and reading from the label.

He shook his head yet again. The effort of not letting fear consume her was in itself threatening to make her crumble. He was deteriorating by the second.

'It's not there,' he managed slowly. He sucked in his breath, as if it pained him to speak.

'Then where *is* it?'

Madeline almost swore, but then realisation struck her like lightning. She cursed at herself. *She* had it—herself. She had put it in her pack that night to keep it safe, after he'd left it in her tent. She'd been intending to give it back to him but she'd forgotten. It was still in the pocket of her pack—which Ryan was now leaning on.

She reached behind him and motioned to the guys to keep him as still as possible while she pulled at the zippers on the pockets. Opening the one on the side, she pulled out the chain with the apple on it that Jason had given her. She'd forgotten to put it back on weeks ago. Then she found the vial she'd shoved in there that night and held it up to him, putting a hand to his clammy face.

'This one? Ryan, please tell me it's this one?'

'Yes,' he managed, wincing again. 'Do it.'

'Me? No, Ryan, you'll have to do it yourself.'

Madeline fumbled to unwrap a syringe. Her mind was screaming at her not to do this. What if it didn't work? What if she didn't do it properly and... God forbid... he died? He was semi-conscious, but *he* could do it. He knew how.

She pulled the top off the vial with trembling fingers and loaded the syringe. The guys were watching her with fear in their eyes.

Ryan reached for her hand. 'You have to do this, Maddy, Stick it right here.'

His breathing was laboured. His eyes kept closing as he held his arm out to her and pointed to a spot in the crease of his elbow. One of the guys held it in place.

'I trust you.'

She had no choice. He was growing greyer by the second.

Madeline took his arm, studied the place he was pointing at for the blue of a vein. 'OK, here goes.'

And before she could think any more about it she stuck the syringe into him and emptied the entire vial.

The next few minutes were a blur. The volunteer, Raul, appeared behind her, hot and flustered. He'd heard her calling, he said, but he'd had his hands full, shifting equipment around, and when he'd tried to find her she had disappeared. He radioed for help, explaining that they now had to get Ryan to the Cessna, which would be waiting for them on the runway when they got up river.

Along with the two local guys, Raul helped to carry Ryan to the boat. He'd passed out.

'Is he going to be OK?' Madeline asked, barely bothering to hide the devastation from her voice as she climbed in alongside them with her bag.

What if she'd got the anti-venom into him too late? What if he didn't make it? What if she lost him?

She couldn't bear it. This jungle was a nightmare—a total nightmare.

'He's just exhausted from trying to stay conscious,' Raul explained. 'We need to get him to the hospital. You probably saved his life, though.'

Tears of relief sprang to her eyes—but he wasn't out of the woods yet, she could tell.

Madeline clung to Ryan's hand as they laid him on the bottom of the boat. He looked like a shadow of his handsome self…so weak and vulnerable. 'I'm so sorry,' she whispered to him as her heart broke, and she crouched beside him, leaning over him, stroking his face.

Raul was frowning, looking at them as he spoke into his radio, and in the back of her mind Madeline knew she was raising suspicion—not that none had been raised concerning the two of them up to this point, she was sure.

She put a hand to his heart now, leant down and kissed

him. *Who cares? So what?* This was her fault. If anything worse happened to this man she knew without a doubt that she would never, ever forgive herself.

CHAPTER NINETEEN

PAIN. THAT WAS all he could feel. Pain and a tightness in his chest that felt a lot as if someone had stomped on him. A nurse was filling in some papers beside him when he opened his eyes, but a millisecond later he noticed someone else in the room, sitting on a plastic chair in the corner beneath the harsh, artificial light.

'Maddy,' he croaked.

He was weak. His leg and foot were bandaged, and he was wearing an ugly white gown, but he was alive. He had *her* to thank for that.

He saw her eyes flutter open, watched her rub them sleepily.

'She never left your side, Dr Ryan,' the elderly nurse said in a thick Portuguese accent, touching a hand to his shoulder as Madeline approached them. 'How do you feel?'

'Yes, how do you feel?' Madeline echoed, concern etched all over her features.

She was extraordinarily tanned, he realised now, in this brand-new setting away from the jungle. She was thinner, too, but so, so beautiful. He didn't deserve her.

'I'm OK,' he replied, looking into her sea-green eyes, feeling far from it.

Madeline reached for his hand and they both watched the nurse walk out of the room and shut the door.

'I owe you my life,' he said as soon as she was gone.

'Then I guess we're even.' She smiled, pulling his hand up to her mouth and kissing the back of it. 'I'm so glad you're OK.' Her eyes were tired and watery. Her hair was piled on the top of her head. 'You scared me, Ryan. I'm so sorry...if I hadn't been acting so crazy—'

'You had every right to act like that,' he interrupted, patting the bed at his side. 'I pushed you to it.'

She sat down. In the harsh light everything seemed clearer, somehow. His thoughts, her actions, the words he knew he had to say... She'd been right before. It had been going on long enough.

'Josephine was in love with me,' he said, before he could think any further.

Madeline's eyes widened, but she didn't let go of his hand. 'I had a feeling she might have been,' she whispered.

Ryan kept his voice steady and low, reliving the memories as he spoke and ploughing onwards anyway. 'But I didn't love *her*, Maddy, not in the same way.'

He moved his eyes to the spotless white ceiling as shame washed through him, as usual.

'We'd been dating in secret for a while—it was all kind of spontaneous and fun, you know? We argued about it... the fact that I could never admit we were a couple. We were arguing when she ran off...that's *why* she ran off.'

'What happened?'

Madeline's eyes were watery, he could see, but she wasn't clearing away her tears. Her fingers were gripping his like a vice.

'She ran into the damn jungle...got herself lost. We couldn't find her.'

'Oh, my God, Ryan…'

'It took four days. She didn't mean for it to happen… she was emotional and she got lost, ended up injuring herself, probably stumbling around in the maze of the jungle. By the time we found her there had been too much blood loss and no one could save her.'

He closed his eyes, feeling his hand grow hotter in hers. He couldn't even expand on the blood loss—it was still too raw.

'Mark and Even knew about us. They warned me to keep things quiet—they didn't want any extra attention from the media affecting the team—and of course I agreed with that. I didn't want the attention either. And then, when it happened…'

'I can imagine!'

'There were so many interviews, Maddy. Josephine didn't have any close family, or much of a life outside the crew, but obviously the world wanted to know what had happened to her. It was too late to tell the whole truth— that we'd been sleeping together and the reason she'd run away was because we'd been arguing about our re-lationship status, of all things… How could I admit that being with her in the first place had been a mistake on my part? I loved the fun we were having, but not enough to tell the world we were a couple. She thought we'd get married. But I was twenty-seven…she was twenty-eight.'

'Ryan, it's OK. I won't write any of this down, I swear.'

'I'm an asshole.'

'You're not—you were young. You just got carried away. You would have done the right thing in the end if you didn't want to marry her. You would have broken it off and gone your separate ways. Neither of you knew she was going to get lost, or what was going to happen in the jungle. People make mistakes. You have to forgive yourself. You *have* to let this go.'

'How can I?'

Madeline put a hand to his face, forced him to look at her. 'Just *choose* to, Ryan. Please. Just *choose* to forgive yourself. You get to start again. You get to be in love for *real*, if you want. You get to say I love you and mean it, and you get to hear it back. You don't have to deny yourself anything out of guilt or shame. I know that's what you've been doing.'

His heart lurched as she leaned in and kissed him softly on the lips, stroking his cheek and stubble. He leaned into her hand.

'I can imagine how awful that must have been for you,' she said. She touched her nose to his. 'It doesn't change the fact that I love you.'

He froze.

Madeline pulled back to meet his eyes as the silence stretched on and on and on. He watched her face change as the words played over and over in his head. Why couldn't he reply? Why couldn't he say anything?

He cleared his throat, searching her eyes. His head was spinning. 'Maddy, I...' He trailed off, letting the words hover in the space between them like heavy weights, waiting for someone to catch them.

And then he left those words to drop and burn themselves out as Evan and Mark entered the room with pretty much the entire crew of *Medical Extremes* and another cameraman.

They had balloons.

CHAPTER TWENTY

Three weeks later

MADELINE STARED OUT at the cold London rain. So different from the rain in the Amazon, she thought. The rain there had been harsh, but warm, and when it ended its assault it would trade places willingly with the sun, sending apologies down in hot white beams. Here it was just endless and mean, and the grey skies held no promise of swooping blue butterflies or lovemaking trysts with Ryan Tobias in waterfalls.

'Coffee?' the waitress asked, stopping at her table with a pot of sloshing brown liquid.

'Sure—thanks.' Madeline held out her cup.

Maybe coffee would cure her writer's block. She was stuck on how to end the memoir. She had over ninety thousand words already, and had thrown herself into writing pretty much the moment the plane had touched down in London. She'd had to—not least because Samantha was already on her back for the manuscript.

Typing about him every day, putting his history together like puzzle pieces on the page, was sheer torture. She missed him as she'd miss a vital organ—felt as if someone had amputated a limb. She couldn't get his face out of her head, nor his words when he'd finally opened up to her in that hospital room.

She remembered what he'd told her, word for haunting word, but knew she could never write it down. Of course she couldn't. Instead her mind played over the words she'd had to swallow when the team had walked in with their balloons.

Balloons. Ryan needed more than balloons to take his pain away. But he didn't *want* anyone to take his pain away—that was the problem. He thought he was destined to live out his days alone, racked with guilt about Josephine. He hadn't loved Josephine. And he'd refused to let anyone love *him* ever since.

Maybe he would never love anyone. Maybe he'd forgotten what love was.

She picked up her coffee, stared out at the honking traffic, thinking back over the flight she'd taken back home from Rio, knowing he was still there in that hospital the whole time. Knowing it was probably over between them. Knowing she was speeding further and further away from him in every sense.

Even so, she needed a better ending for him—something to inspire joy in other people the way he had in her.

Madeline had been accepted back at St David's and was already picking up where she'd left off. The same faces with the same smiles had been so understanding, so welcoming and helpful. She almost felt as though she'd never left.

Almost.

She put her cup down, sank back against the booth and let her eyes fall on the blank page on her screen. Her writing skills were all she had to give Ryan now, and she couldn't let them all be for nothing. She had no clue how she was going to finish the memoir, but she knew she had to find a way. She could write, and she could help others, and with more book deals at her fingertips—if she ever had time outside her nursing duties—she had the power to combine both.

She knew in her heart that she wasn't the same nurse who'd left St David's after Toby had died. An indelible line had been drawn between the old her and the new one. The new Madeline had taken risks and chances, had put herself in the line of fire and witnessed incredible things. The new Madeline had survived seemingly endless days on rice and fruit, learned how to trust in her own abilities and instincts, gained the respect of a tribe of children who sang from their hearts about the simplest of life's precious gifts, like butterflies and bananas and toothbrushes.

The new Madeline had felt love of the highest, most soul-splintering kind, spilling into her heart and filling the spaces there. She'd been lifted and bolstered by it—so much so that its absence hadn't killed her. She was still kind of floating. Perhaps a little bruised and unsure, but definitely grateful for a taste of what she now knew was out there.

Maybe she could find it again with someone else.

CHAPTER TWENTY-ONE

RYAN PUSHED THROUGH the door, feeling sweat break out on his forehead as soon as he stopped short under the bright, unforgiving lights. A woman in a tracksuit and neon pink sneakers seemed to recognise him instantly. Her eyes widened and she stopped in her tracks, looking as though she was about to race over to him in excitement.

Ryan held up his hand and hurried on past, pulling his baseball hat down further over his forehead.

He'd tossed and turned last night in his hotel room, debating whether or not to come, but Mark and Evan had finally sat him down at breakfast, shoved a black coffee under his nose and then given him another, perhaps even more effective wake-up call.

'She's the best thing that's ever happened to you!'

'With all due respect, Ryan, don't screw this up!'

'You *know*?' he'd said, feigning surprise.

You couldn't live that closely with people and not understand that they'd know when you were hiding something.

'It's been written all over your face ever since you first set eyes on each other. You're the smartest guy in the field, Ryan, but really you're an idiot.'

This room smelled of astringent fluids and the shiny floor squeaked under his sneakers. Anxiety crept tighter around him like a rope. Seeing a reception desk, he made his way over. A girl of about twenty-one with a name badge reading 'Trudy' looked up, then did a double-take.

'Oh,' she said when he met her eyes. 'You.'

'I'm looking for Nurse Madeline Savoia. I was told she's here today?'

'Um…yeah…um…lemme just look that up…' Trudy trailed off, dropping a pen to the floor as she scrambled nervously for some papers.

Ryan tried not to smile and rested an arm on the counter. He was still getting used to people acting this way around him again. No one in the Amazon gave a toss who he was as long as he could help when someone needed him. If only the whole world cared more about those things…

He looked around him as a flummoxed Trudy scanned her computer screen. People in scrubs were walking alongside kids of all ages in gowns with dressings and gauzes. Parents and other relatives were milling about, lost in their phones and magazines. An elderly man was wiping up a coffee spillage by a vending machine. A young couple each holding a pile of kids' books looked at him with vague recollection, presumably trying to figure out where they'd seen him.

In his Red Sox shirt and jeans, Ryan looked like any other regular guy. Well, maybe an American. He wondered what people would do when they found out what he was planning—just as soon as he could locate Madeline.

'She's on Peter Pan Ward… No, sorry…they moved her group to Elephant and Giraffe today.' Trudy was beetroot-red now, fiddling with the braid that she'd pulled across her shoulder.

'Sorry?' he said. 'Elephant and Giraffe?'

Was this some kind of zoo?

'It's the haematology/oncology department.' She stood up, pointing a manicured finger down the hallway. 'She should still be there somewhere, if you go through those doors and take a right.'

'Right. Thank you.'

'Wait—Ryan, can you please sign this? I really love *Medical Extremes*…it's, like, my favourite show. And my mum's, too.' She pushed a piece of paper and a blue pen onto the desk, blushing even more.

'What's your mum's name?' he asked, taking the pen. He figured he needed all the good karma he could get.

'Sandy.'

He signed the paper—*To Sandy, love Ryan*—and added a heart, throwing Trudy a wink he knew would make her day.

Then, before anyone else could approach him, he walked quickly down the corridor and hurried through the double doors.

His thoughts were a washing machine on spin cycle as he walked the length of the ward, narrowly missing being struck by a toddler on a tiny tricycle. He'd never been this nervous in his life.

It had been the longest few weeks ever since she'd left him in that hospital in Rio. Her face had haunted him… that look in her eyes as he'd choked on his reply to her confession.

Fear had started rolling over him like waves from a tsunami the second she'd said what she had.

Did she *really* love him? Did he love *her*?

He'd watched her leave that hospital room, felt the ball of knots twist tighter in his stomach. Mark and Evan and everyone else had crowded around him with the balloons and he'd said nothing—just watched the back of her head and her hand sweep across her hidden face as she'd turned towards the door.

He'd needed to get his head around it. When they'd all gone, however, Ryan had felt as alone in that busy hospital as he had in the middle of the jungle at night. But in spite of the silence he had ached with the noises in his head.

He'd kept the truth locked inside some damn pointless Pandora's Box for so long that saying them hadn't felt real. Yet the words about Josephine had come out, no matter what Madeline chose to do with them. It hadn't been the thought of what she'd do with them that had plagued him, though. It had been the thought of losing her again.

All night he'd lain awake, his heart pounding as he'd healed. Visions of her smiling, laughing, floating in the lake had messed with his senses. He had almost smelled her, tasted her. Every movement she'd made in his arms, every molecule of Madeline, had seemed imprinted on his brain like a tattoo.

He'd wanted to get up and follow her, to catch her before she flew away, but as strong as his emotions were, and—dare he say it?—as strong as his love…his body was weak.

He loved Madeline, too. Of course he did. What was not to love? And who cared about a stupid memoir or what anyone else might think?

The people he was so concerned about were all just skin and blood and bones, living in the same jungle as him. He was just like everyone else in the world—doing his best to survive. Some survived longer than others, that was all. Josephine had run into trouble, but ultimately her death was not his fault—just as Toby's wasn't Madeline's.

He also knew he couldn't have forced love to exist

where it hadn't back then. He'd been young and confused, of course, chasing adventure and fun. Josephine had made him happy in that moment—and perhaps he had been selfish. But what he'd felt for Josephine was nothing compared to what he'd grown to feel for Madeline.

Why should he deny himself happiness now? Why shouldn't he be allowed to say *I love you* to someone, and mean it?

He'd known even as he'd boarded the flight what he wanted to do.

Now minutes passed like hours as he searched the waiting room, the mini-cafeteria, the playroom.

Please, God, just don't let her tell me where to shove it. Then...

It was the back of her head he saw first. He stopped and peeked through a window into the last in a long row of rooms leading off the corridor. He'd have recognised her anywhere. The soft slope of her shoulders in her blue scrubs...the knot of hair pinned to the top of her head.

He looked around him, then back into the room. There was one bed with a kid in it—no older than eleven or twelve. Madeline was talking to her, sitting on the bed, facing away from him. He could hear the TV on the wall, the faint, jovial preposterousness of a cartoon.

He put his hand on the door handle and before he could chicken out walked inside.

The little girl's head was bald, making her big blue eyes appear even wider as she gasped.

'Dr Ryan Tobias?' she exclaimed in disbelief.

Madeline froze. On the TV a cartoon mouse screamed with perfect timing.

'Is it really you?' the little girl asked, blinking and sitting up straighter in the bed.

He saw a card on the dresser that read *Get well soon, Camille*.

Madeline still didn't turn around.

His heart was thudding now. 'Yes, Camille, it's really me,' he said, letting his eyes fall on Madeline as he shut the door behind him.

'What are you doing here? Is this a dream?'

He smiled at her. Out of the corner of his eye he saw Madeline's face had turned pale, and she'd closed her eyes, lowered her head to her chest.

'It's not a dream,' he said softly, walking to the side of her bed. He was opposite Madeline now. 'I'm here to see your friend, and to tell her I've been really, really stupid.'

The girl giggled, seeming younger than eleven or twelve. 'You're not stupid! I've seen you on the telly!'

'Well, sometimes, Camille, I do stupid things that you don't see on the telly,' he said.

'Like what?'

He paused for a moment, then reached his hand across the bed to rest it on Madeline's shoulder. 'Like letting this amazing woman fly away on a plane without me.'

Madeline opened her eyes. She brought her hand up slowly to cover his and he swore he saw a tear trickle down her nose.

'Oh, my God, do you *love* Nurse Madeline?' Camille asked, eyes wide in excitement.

'Yes, I do,' he replied, conscious now of a group of people crowding at the window, looking at them from behind the glass. 'Very much. Nurse Madeline is a very special woman.'

'Yes, she is,' Camille replied quickly. 'But I can't believe it's really you.'

Madeline stood up and clocked all the people watching

them. For a moment he wanted to yank the blind down, but then he figured, *What the hell?*

He met her at the end of the bed and took her hands. They were warm and slightly clammy. She had tears streaming down her cheeks now.

'What are you doing here?' she choked.

'Don't cry,' he whispered, wiping her tears away with his thumbs.

'I don't know what to say...'

'Don't say anything.'

He dropped to his knees, fumbling in his pocket on the way to the cold floor. He heard her gasp audibly. So did Camille, and the noise levels behind the window went up a notch.

'I love you, Madeline, that's all I came to say...and as well to ask you one important question.'

'Ryan, what are you...?'

'I knew I was in love with you the minute I almost lost you—when I thought that dead body was you. Probably even before that...'

'Ryan...'

'I can't live without you. I really can't. In fact, I refuse to. I want you to marry me. *Will* you marry me, Madeline Savoia?'

Madeline let out a sudden laugh as tears continued to stream down her face.

'Are you serious?'

He smiled up at her. 'Serious as a snakebite.'

'In that case I say yes!' She clutched at his hands holding hers. *'Yes!'*

He got up, took her hand in his, and she stared in disbelief at the ring he was sliding on her finger, its stunning diamond catching the light.

'Oh, my God—my friends will never believe this.' Camille was reaching for her phone, taking a photo.

Ryan didn't care. Let her Tweet about it.

'Ryan? Is this what you want?'

Madeline was looking from the ring to him, as if she might at any moment see a camera sweep in and pronounce her 'punked'.

He let out a laugh that felt like a dead weight falling from his shoulders and dropped another kiss on her lips—which she returned until they were kissing passionately in the middle of the room and everyone outside was whooping and cheering.

When he pulled away, holding a hand up at the window, he heard Camille clapping enthusiastically behind them.

'You know, I didn't exactly want to be in here,' she blurted from the bed, 'but I wouldn't have missed this moment for anything. So you're marrying *the* Dr Ryan Tobias, Nurse Madeline?'

Madeline shook her head for a second. 'I guess I am...' she said.

Ryan pulled her against him, once again breathing in the scent he'd missed. 'I hope that's true—because the second I walk out of this room I'll be mobbed, and I'll probably need my fiancée to save me.'

The words sounded strange coming from his mouth. He was planning a real future with Madeline and he was actually excited about it. There was so much he wanted to say, and even more he wanted to do... But not with Camille in the same room.

He cleared his throat. 'When do you finish your shift?'

'Not till seven...'

'Meet me at the Shangri La. We need to talk about things. We also need to talk about this memoir.'

'Ryan, I got pretty far, but then I stopped writing it...'

'Well, you need to start again,' he said, letting her go and putting his hand on the doorknob. He could hear more people outside gathering, talking, gossiping, gasping. 'I need you to get that story out there for the good of *both* of us. I'll call your editor and tell her why the manuscript is late. I'll explain that I wouldn't give you an ending, but now I'm going to write that part myself and send it to you. I want my memoir to have a *happy* ending—you hear?'

She shook her head, confused.

He kissed her lips, pressed his forehead to hers. 'I'm going to say that, thanks to an irritating, relentless but irresistible nurse, who saved his life in the Amazon, Ryan Tobias met the love of his life. And maybe a little bit more than that. But you can't edit that bit, OK?'

'OK...'

'Good. Now, I'm heading out there. If you hear a desperate scream it's just me.'

'I'll come and save you—I promise,' she said, smiling through her tears.

'That's what you do best,' he replied, and grinned.

EPILOGUE

Afterword from Flying High,
a memoir by Dr Ryan Tobias.

As I TYPE my way towards the end of this book—a book I urge you to remember I didn't even want written—I'm feeling a sense of peace I never expected to feel.

I've thought a lot about why this is, and I think it's because when you acknowledge why you don't want to do something…when you really face that demon head on… you realise that what is really bothering you is yourself— and yourself is something you can change in a heartbeat.

You just have to want to.

I'm making some big changes in my life, and I'm not afraid to say that falling in love has helped me make them. The wonderful woman you've probably seen me out with has changed the way I see myself and consequently the way I see the world! There was a time when I didn't dare think I deserved such a love, or such a wedding, filled with so many friends, colleagues and people I love. Maybe you saw the photos? Then you'll know I'm a lucky man indeed.

Oh, and if you didn't think it was possible for this flying doctor's life to get any more adventurous, believe me, you're not alone. Let's just say we've been busy painting one of our rooms a lovely shade of blue, and my wife has recently commented that she can no longer fit into her favourite jeans.

It's a beautiful thing, knowing a whole new life is about to begin, and I sincerely hope you'll come along with us for the ride.

Till the next adventure!

Yours,

Ryan Tobias.

PS Please note: all proceeds from this book's sales are to be split between St David's Hospital Elephant and Giraffe Wards and the Ryan Tobias Foundation. Thank you for your support.

* * * * *

MILLS & BOON

Coming next month

BOUND BY THEIR BABIES
Caroline Anderson

People joked all the time about sex-crazed widows, and there was no way—*no way*—she was turning into one! This was *Jake*, for heaven's sake! Her friend. Not her lover. Not her boyfriend. And certainly not someone for a casual one-nighter.

Although they'd almost gone there that once, and the memory of the awkwardness that had followed when they'd come to their senses and pulled away from the brink had never left her, although it had long been buried.

Until now…

Emily heard the stairs creak again, and pressed down the plunger and slid the pot towards him as he came into the room.

'Here, your coffee.'

'Aren't you having any?'

She shook her head, but she couldn't quite meet his eyes, and she realised he wasn't looking at her, either. 'I'll go back up in case Zach cries and wakes Matilda. Don't forget to ring me when you've seen Brie.'

'OK. Thanks for making the coffee.'

'You're welcome. Have a good day.'

She tiptoed up the stairs, listened for the sound of the front door closing and watched him from his bedroom window as he walked briskly down the road towards the hospital, travel mug in hand.

He turned the corner and went out of sight, and she sat down on the edge of his bed, her fingers knotting in a handful of rumpled bedding. *What was she doing?* With a stifled scream of frustration, she fell sideways onto the mattress and buried her face in his duvet.

Mistake. She could smell the scent of him on the sheets, warm and familiar and strangely exciting, could picture that glorious nakedness stretched out against the stark white linen, a beautiful specimen of masculinity in its prime—

She jack-knifed to her feet. This was crazy. What on earth had happened to her? They'd been friends for years, and now all of a sudden this uncontrollable urge to sniff his sheets?

They had to keep this platonic. So much was riding on it—their mutual careers, if nothing else!

And the children—they had to make this work for the children, especially Matilda. The last thing she needed—any of them needed—was this fragile status quo disrupted for anything as trivial as primitive, adolescent lust.

It wasn't fair on any of them, and she'd embarrassed herself enough fifteen years ago. She wasn't doing it again.

No way.

Continue reading
BOUND BY THEIR BABIES
Caroline Anderson

Available next month
www.millsandboon.co.uk

LET'S TALK
Romance

For exclusive extracts, competitions
and special offers, find us online:

- facebook.com/millsandboon
- @millsandboonuk
- @millsandboon

Or get in touch on 0844 844 1351*

For all the latest titles coming soon, visit
millsandboon.co.uk/nextmonth